REBELLIOUS SURRENDER

THE SURRENDER SERIES, BOOK TWO

ZOE BLAKE

Poison Ink Publications

Copyright © 2018, 2021 by Zoe Blake & Poison Ink Publications

All rights reserved.
No part of this book may be reproduced in any form or by any electronic or mechanical means, including information storage and retrieval systems, without written permission from the author, except for the use of brief quotations in a book review.

Cover Design by Dark City Designs

CONTENTS

Chapter 1	1
Chapter 2	12
Chapter 3	21
Chapter 4	32
Chapter 5	45
Chapter 6	56
Chapter 7	71
Chapter 8	80
Chapter 9	92
Chapter 10	104
Chapter 11	111
Chapter 12	123
About Zoe Blake	131
Also by Zoe Blake	133

CHAPTER 1

She had been a thief most of her life; tonight, she would become a killer.

The night was still and peaceful.

Surveying the quiet city street, she was careful to stay within the shadows.

He had chosen his safe house well. It was just on the edge of Potomac Park in D.C. The small, unassuming brick house was moments away from Independence Avenue which would allow a quick getaway to the highways. Plus, it skirted the edge of the Yards, a low-rent, high crime area. The perfect place to score equipment, a quick smash-and-grab crew or fake I.D.s from people who didn't ask a lot of bothersome questions. Of course, that was why he was considered the best.

They called him Paine. Doubtful it was his real name. None of them used their real names. Real names were for people with families, memories, and normal jobs, a real life. In her world, there was only the moment. The adrenaline rush of a heist. The pride in a good score. Living for the day because tomorrow was not a promise. In her world, trust was a fantasy of the foolish and love was a weakness. Too bad she had forgotten all that, allowed herself to trust and fall in love, to actually believe she could have a chance at a normal life.

Then Paine took it all away from her.

Killed the man she loved.

And now he would pay.

First, she took away the only thing of real value any criminal had—their reputation. But it was not enough. It should have been. Watching him get burned, not knowing who had set him up. Watching him twist and spin as her web closed tighter and tighter around him.

It had all been perfect. The perfect setup. The perfect deception. The perfect revenge.

She could feel the warm stone between her breasts. The Raj Pink diamond. The thirty-seven-carat diamond he'd been hired to steal.

She'd gotten there first.

She'd stolen the diamond and let The Syndicate, the crime outfit they both worked for, believe Paine had double-crossed them. She had been thorough, posting on the dark web to make it look like Paine was searching for a buyer. Then she'd started dropping hints among the dirty dealers that he had sold fake jewels and artwork to them over the years and that Paine's reputation as a master thief was a sham.

The final piece was returning a Vermeer to a museum in Brussels that he had stolen from it and sold two years ago. Except the Vermeer the museum got back was an exceptionally well-done fraud. Not that the museum cared. They primly ignored the signs and announced the triumphant return of their masterpiece, while Paine's underworld and very influential buyer seethed. Assuming he had been deceived by Paine, he was demanding his five million back. The best part was, assuming it was of no value, the underworld buyer had practically tossed the original Vermeer aside, placing it in storage at one of his estates. She had snatched it up with no problem. It now graced her walls in her London flat. A reminder of her perfect revenge on Paine.

It really had all been perfect. The perfect setup. The perfect deception. The perfect revenge.

She waited for the final climax. The final act.

She had hoped The Syndicate would put out a contract on him. Hoped they would do her dirty work for her, finish the job she had started and kill him for his betrayal. A fitting end.

Impatiently, she'd watched and waited, listening for rumors or even a hint someone had been hired to kill Paine. Nothing.

Criminals had short memories, especially when a big score was involved. Instead of a kill contract, she began to hear murmurings that Paine was returning. A man of his special skills was hard to find. A trained fighter, thief and hacker. A criminal Renaissance man. The Syndicate was beginning to doubt Paine had betrayed them.

Now her perfect plan was unraveling.

With Paine back in The Syndicate's good graces, he

would have the resources to learn it was she who had betrayed him. He was a dangerous man to cross. Their brief past connection would mean nothing to him. He would kill her for certain, slowly and painfully, for her deception. That was, if The Syndicate didn't get to her first. They would not take too kindly to learning she had set up one of their best operatives. Despite her skills as a master thief and almost cult-like reputation, Paine was worth more to them.

She needed to act fast. She would kill Paine and plant the diamond on him. The Syndicate would be assured of his betrayal and move on.

She would be safe and her final revenge realized, by her own hand.

It had taken her months to track him down to this safe house. Another month of careful surveillance, each day worrying he would pick up and leave.

Now her time was up. The Syndicate had ordered her to London to perform a job for them. No one told The Syndicate no.

She would have to put her plan into action tonight.

It would be perfect. The perfect setup. The perfect deception. The perfect revenge.

The perfect murder.

* * *

KEEPING TO THE DARK, she hurried along to the back of the house. Placing her knapsack on the ground, she pulled out her CPM-700. The counter-surveillance probe would let her know if Paine had installed any new cameras or audio devices other than the ones she had already mapped out on a floor plan of his house. Crouching low, she turned on the small black box, waving the handheld wand over the house and surrounding area. All the electronic noise was coming from the lower level. Paine was either careless or arrogant, leaving the upstairs unprotected with any kind of electronic eavesdropping devices. Opening up the four flukes of her foldable, steel grappling hook, she drew out the slack on the rope and chain. Throwing back her arm, she swung the hook in a circle, picking up speed. Finally, she let it fly, watching through the darkness as it arced before hitting its mark, the balcony under the second-story window. She winced at the slight screeching noise the hook made as it connected with the balcony, followed by the hollow clang of the chain as it wrapped around the stone balustrade. The chain was loud but necessary. It would withstand the rough rubbing along the rock better than the rope which could fray and break.

Creeping under the cover of a low-branched tree she waited, holding her breath to see if the subtle yet unmistakable sound of the grappling hook had alerted her quarry. She knew better than to watch for a sudden light in the window. A trained criminal like Paine would know not to give away his position or the fact that he had been alerted. No, her first warning would be a shot fired at close range or perhaps the thrust of a knife between her ribs to pierce her lungs and prevent her from screaming for help. He wasn't called Paine by accident.

Feeling her legs tingle and cramp from her crouched position, still she waited. Searching the stillness for any sign of movement.

Finally, she was satisfied it was safe to proceed.

Securing the knapsack to her back, she grabbed the rope and placed her toe in the first foothold. She had created a bowline with a bight knot every foot and a half to make her climb easy and quick. In a matter of seconds, she was tossing a leg over the balustrade. Peering through the glass into the darkness, she saw the faint outlines of a bed, dresser and chair. This was the spare bedroom. She knew from her surveillance that Paine slept in the front bedroom. It was easier to monitor the street that way. Cops came through the front. Only criminals came through the back.

Even currently being on the outs with The Syndicate, Paine had a fearsome reputation. Any criminal would have to be mad…or determined…or both…to try to harm him. It was no wonder he didn't bother with any extreme security measures for the safe house, that and it would draw the attention of curious neighbors to see the blinking red lights of cameras and a satellite dish on what should be a ramshackle house with a lower income owner.

She was on a narrow balcony meant more for show than leisure, so there wasn't a patio door with a lock she could easily pick. Only three large windows, side by side, overlooking the garden. Once again reaching into her knapsack, she took out her roll of butcher paper. Unrolling a large sheet, she placed it against the window for measurement, using a razor to cut it to size. Reaching into her knapsack, she grabbed a small, brown glass bottle. Cringing at the smell when she unscrewed the metal cap, she pulled free the small brush, careful to watch the gooey streams of glue. Gingerly brushing the paper with the rubber cement, she lifted it up and adhered it to the window. Using her watch, since the glow from a phone could alert someone to her presence, she waited several minutes for the glue to dry. Unlike what the movies showed, successful breaking and entering was about stealth and patience. The faster you worked, the louder you were likely to be.

Testing a corner of the paper, she was satisfied it was fully adhered to the glass window. Taking out her pocket-sized brass hammer, she gave the window a strong tap right in the center. It shattered. Moving quickly, she caught the now heavy piece of butcher paper before it fell to the ground. A breaking window did not actually make much sound. It was the sound of glass shards hitting the floor that made all the noise. With the large pieces stuck to the butcher paper, there was only the slightest tinkling sound from the falling remnants. Cautious not to cut herself or, worse, disturb the jagged pieces that still lined the sill, she reached in to unlock the window. Slowly, she raised the sash. The sound of metal scraping against stone from the grappling hook was far worse than the muted sound of wood sliding along wood but still, it was noise. Any noise could alert him to her presence.

Again, she waited, holding her breath, training her ear for any sound that would indicate movement inside. At the slightest sign of trouble, she would be over the balcony and down the rope, becoming a mist among the shadows before anyone got close enough to see her face.

All was still.

It was time.

Reaching once more into her bag of tools, she pulled out the one thing she usually never carried on a heist. A gun.

She was a thief, not a murderer. Her tools of the trade were flush cutters, cone steel bits and lock pick sets. If there was danger, she fled.

Except for tonight.

Everything was different tonight.

Instead of fleeing danger, she was walking headlong into it. Six feet and two inches of hard muscle danger. It was a wonder he was so successful as a thief with all that brawn. Thieves were usually small and wiry like her. It was probably why he'd developed a reputation for...other things. He didn't flee when caught. He stood his ground and fought his way out. Whereas she got her information through research and observance when on a job, Paine was known for the more direct approach, extracting it from unwilling participants. Once again she was reminded that he wasn't called Paine by accident.

Ruthlessly stifling a shudder and shaking off dreadful premonitions, she continued with her plan. This was for Dev, she thought.

With her Ruger .22 in hand, she screwed on the barrel extender, the suppressor. This was a quiet neighborhood. She didn't want to alert the police any sooner than necessary. The silencer would buy her time.

Leery of falling glass, she made sure not to jostle the

frame as she stepped through the window into the dark interior.

Deftly circling around the furniture, she crept out of the room into the hallway.

Pausing for a moment, she tried to slow her racing heart. She needed to stay calm and focused.

Despite wanting to rush and get it over with, she had to proceed slowly. Now that she was inside the home, there were several unknowns. There was a hardwood floor. Any board could let out a telltale squeak, giving both her position and presence away. It was why she always wore dance sneakers. With their split, soft rubber soles meant for sliding across dance floors, they were ideal.

Sliding her foot along the boards, testing each before placing her full weight into her step, she made slow and steady progress down the hallway to his ajar bedroom door.

Holding her breath, she stopped when she was at the threshold. All was silent and still.

Bracing the gun with both hands, she stretched out her arms and crossed the threshold.

The glow through the gossamer curtains from the streetlight outside allowed her to just make out the shape of the bed and the long form under the covers.

The tip of her finger caressed the trigger. Her hand started to shake. She tightened her grip under the butt to steady her shooting hand.

Tears briefly clouded her vision, but she blinked them away. Knowing at any moment he could wake and find her standing over his bed with a gun, she had reached the point of no return.

Sucking in a steadying breath, she pulled the trigger.

There was a faint thwap sound before a spray of tiny white feathers flew into the air. Dismayed, she stepped toward the bed and threw back the covers. It was empty, save for a pile of strategically placed pillows.

From the corner of the room came a low, mirthless chuckle.

She turned, gun raised, peering into the shadows. The dark outline of a tall form stepped forward.

"I honestly didn't think you would have the balls to do it."

Her jaw clenched. Her lips felt stiff and unresponsive as she forced them to form that one single word. "Paine." She uttered it like a curse.

"Hello, Mirage. Welcome to my home," he intoned with a mock bow.

With a cry, she fired the gun again but not before he swung right, knocking her outstretched arm with his hand. Plaster dust rained down on them both as the bullet glanced across the ceiling. Placing his large hand over her smaller ones, he wrenched the gun from her grasp, tossing it onto the bed as he spun her around. Her back connected with his front. His free arm forced hers down, pinning them against her body.

He whispered darkly into her ear, "I knew if I waited and made myself enough of a target, the person who set me up would strike again."

Mirage felt sick with fear. Her knees buckled, but his restraining arm kept her upright.

"I'm going to make you pay." His sharp teeth nipped at the delicate curve of her ear as Paine hissed his malicious threat.

Mirage closed her eyes.

Clasped in Paine's strong, unrelenting grasp, she knew…she was a dead woman.

CHAPTER 2

Still, she wasn't going down without a fight.

Straining her neck to the left, she sank her teeth into the flesh of his upper arm. He released her with a roar. Mirage bolted through the door with Paine hard on her heels. There was a hard blow to her lower back. Losing her balance, she crashed to the wooden hallway floor. Half crawling, half running, she struggled to raise herself up. Strong fingers clasped around her ankle. Turning on her back, she kicked out at him, connecting with his jaw, desperate to be free. Dodging her flailing limb, he grabbed her other ankle and pulled. She slid along the polished surface till her open legs straddled his knees. Releasing her ankles, he placed a hand on either side of her head.

"Keep struggling. It will make fucking you all that much more fun," he laughed.

Mirage scratched her nails down his cheek before scrambling backward when he was momentarily distracted. Flipping over, she launched herself upright and ran. Recognizing that the window entrance to the second bedroom was too narrow and that the additional time it would take her to maneuver over the balustrade and down the rope would cost her precious seconds, Mirage knew the front door was her only hope. Stumbling down the stairs, skipping several at a time, her body bounced between the wall and the railing in her haste. Upon reaching the front foyer, she flattened both palms against the door to stop her momentum. Reaching down, she scrambled for the knob while scrabbling for the key with her other hand.

Hands encircled the tops of her shoulders, spinning her around, slamming her back against the door.

Even in the darkness, she could make out the harsh angles and fierce outline of his face.

"Just tell me why, Mira?" he ground out. There was an element of hurt in his voice which confused Mirage.

Bending her knees to break his grasp, she ducked under his arm and ran blindly. Her shin bumped into a low table. Scanning the space, she realized she must be in the living room. Remembering the floor plan despite her frenzy, she turned left knowing beyond was the dining room then the kitchen. Through the kitchen was the back door and her last chance at freedom.

Just as she could make out the wide, rectangular shape of the dining room table, an arm wrapped around her stomach from behind. She screamed, grabbing for the high-backed chair at the head of the table for purchase, the only thing she could reach. The heavy chair toppled backward as she was pulled back into the living room.

Her only choice now was the police. If the neighbors

awoke from the sounds of her screams and the struggle, they would probably call them. The police would question her presence in the house. They would undoubtedly find her knapsack filled with burglary tools. It would also place Paine in an awkward position. He wouldn't want to tell the police too many details about himself and their prior relationship. He would be forced to say she was just a stranger. An opportunistic housebreaker. It meant possible prison time, but at least she would be alive.

Sucking in a fevered gasp for another scream, she never got the chance.

His large hand covered her mouth. The side of his index finger pressed against her nose. Between that and the heavy weight of his arm crushing her ribs and stifling her lungs, her air supply was completely cut off. Mirage struggled for breath as she clawed at his hand.

"Stop and I will let you breathe."

With no other choice, she wilted in his arms.

Paine let her body slide to the floor at his feet. Standing over her, his bare chest was clearly outlined in the dim light. His denim-clad legs spread wide as he stared down at her. He looked like some kind of vengeful god.

Mirage could tell he was assessing the situation. Assessing her. She felt rather than saw his gaze as it scanned her body from head to toe, not missing a single detail. The power of his intense scrutiny stopped at her chest. Looking down, she could see her thin black T-shirt had become torn in the struggle. Glinting in the yellow glow of the streetlight from outside was the Raj Pink diamond, peeking out from between the curves of her breasts.

It sealed her fate.

The tension in the room was thick. Their blood was running high and hot with violence and lust.

With a growl, he fell to his knees. The wide spread of his legs easily spanned her narrow hips. His hands fell to either side of her head, caging her in. Mirage expected to feel the cold grip of his strong hands around her throat, strangling the life out of her.

She was shocked beyond reason when his mouth crashed down on her own.

Taking possession.

His tongue swept in to stop all protest. Shifting, he moved his hand to her breast, palming the soft flesh, digging the tips of his fingers in, marking her with the bruise of his touch. The violence of his kiss crushed her lips against her teeth. He tasted of whiskey and the metallic tang of blood. His hand moved lower, cupping between her legs.

Mirage moaned as her hips shifted upwards.

"Is this what you really came for, baby?" he breathed against her lips.

The harsh sound of his voice brought Mirage back to reality, cutting through the haze of anger and lust.

"No!" she yelled as she tried to push his dominating weight off her. "I hate you. I want you dead!"

Leaning back on his thighs, his hand went to the zipper of his jeans. "Let's see just how much you hate me."

Mirage twisted onto her front and, using her elbows for purchase, tried to shimmy out from between his legs.

Paine grabbed her by the hips and pulled backward.

Forced onto her knees, the front of her body low to the ground, her ass brushed against him. She could feel the hard ridge of his cock press into her flesh. Panicked, Mirage started to clutch at the Persian rug, desperately trying to get away. She couldn't let him know, let him feel, how much he affected her. It was her body not her mind, and she wouldn't give him the satisfaction.

Keeping a restraining hand on her middle, he forced the fingers of his right into the waistband of her black yoga pants. Wrenching her pants down, he exposed her pale skin as the thin fabric bunched around her lower thighs.

"No!" she screamed.

His only response was to press a hand between her shoulder blades, forcing her upper body into the rug, her head to the side. She could hear the metallic trill of his zipper. A faint rustle of fabric.

He leaned over her prone body. "It's not like I haven't fucked this sweet cunt before, Mira. Do you remember that? Remember me spanking this sweet ass and making you scream?"

Mirage squeezed her eyes tightly shut, ignoring his familiar use of the name Mira. His special nickname for her. No one else called her that, just Paine. She tried to force the memory of that warm summer's eve in a foreign land aside. Thinking she was going to die among the bullets and bombs that had rained down on them, she had given in to Paine's seduction. She hated to recall that memory as it had been the most passionate night of her life, far surpassing the ineffective lovemaking of Dev, the man she supposedly loved.

Oh God. Her body jerked at the humiliating remembrance of how she'd responded to him calling her his babygirl. It was kinky and fucked up and so wrong, and she had reveled in every minute of it.

One night. One fucked up night of fucked up sex.

It had ruined everything.

The shadow of Paine had haunted her for Dev's and her entire relationship. Dev never quite lived up to the memory of Paine. Another reason why she hated the man. Although she was with Paine before she dated Dev, her lasting memories of that night always made her feel as if she were cheating.

She could feel his hot flesh touch her chilled skin and the touch of his cock as he let it fall against her ass, caressing her. He reached between her legs and stroked her already wet clit, forcing a response. Her back arched as she pushed her hips back, grinding into his hand.

"You're a bastard for this, you know that?"

"You tried to put a bullet in me. I think it's only fair I put my cock in you, especially since we both know you want it."

Two fingers pulsed as they circled her clit, her hips jerking in response. The scratchy seam of his jeans scraped against her outer thighs. She could smell the astringent, musky scent of his cologne with every inhale. Each sound seemed indistinct and far away through the thrumming in her ears. She felt the brush of his knuckles on the underside curve of her ass as he fisted his cock.

The shaft pushed between her clenched thighs. The bulbous head forced its way to her entrance.

Mirage tried to buck her hips. The movement earned her an open-palmed slap on her right buttock. She screeched in shocked pain as prickling heat radiated from where his hand had connected with her, sending unwanted ripples of illicit sensation between her legs.

"Stop or I will make it worse for you."

What could possibly be worse than this humiliation? Her own body was betraying her, thought Mirage, as the weight of his body covered her own, pinning her down. The confident way he handled her, the power in his tight grasp, even his anger, all started to affect her. Memories of his touch came flooding back.

The head pushed in past the tightly clasped ring of muscle. Her body's feeble, waning resistance to his assault useless.

Shifting his hand to her other hip, Paine rolled his hips back before violently thrusting forward.

The force of his cock pushing deep inside of her drove her body to the ground.

He pulled back, forcing her back onto her knees.

He thrust again.

A moan escaped her lips. She hated the satisfying feeling of fullness as his cock drove inside her.

His thick shaft pierced her in two. Her body burned as it struggled to accept each pulsing thrust.

"No, stop!" she cried out, fighting her body's response as her arms reached weakly back, trying to push him away.

Still he shoved his cock into her body with powerful force.

"Say it. Say it, babygirl," he breathed heavily against her neck. "Say 'fuck me.'"

"Bite me," she rebelliously ground out.

Sharp teeth sunk into the delicate flesh of her neck in retaliation as his large hand palmed her breast through her T-shirt. Disgusted with herself, Mirage wished he was touching her skin, wanted to once again feel the warmth of his hand. She remembered how he liked to pinch her nipples till she cried out in pleasure-tinged pain.

The pressure of his rhythmic thrusts began to build. A spiraling warmth grew in the pit of her stomach. Her thighs clenched as she balled her hands into fists. Her primal self took over. The irrational side. The part of her that gloried in his violent mastery of her body, in his display of masculine power.

The pressure continued to build with each thrust.

Without thinking, she reached between her legs and rubbed her clit. The tips of her fingers brushed the underside of his shaft as he pushed deep.

She felt rather than heard the rumble of his groan.

He thrust faster. Her whole frame rocked from the force of it.

Mirage fell forward, her arms stretched out, her fingers splayed wide as her body tensed for one supreme moment. Then her world splintered into a chaos of light, sound and color.

She was only dimly aware of his continued thrusts into her now-sensitive cunt before she heard his roar. Felt the warmth of his come on her lower back. The heat of his body as he collapsed along her side.

The night was once again still, but its peace was shattered.

CHAPTER 3

*P*aine focused on the tactile.

The feel of her soft body against his own. The brush of one of her errant, silky blonde curls as it laid against his shoulder. The sound of her breathing. The harsh feel of the floor.

Anything to focus him. Anything to quiet the primal rage still coursing through his veins.

For months he had been searching for the person who had burned him. One didn't live the type of life he did without making enemies. The thing was, his enemies were usually the brute-force type. The kind that came at you in dark alleys with knives.

He was a criminal Renaissance man. The type of man who could pull off any job, no matter the danger or risk. His specialty was art theft, but he was also used as a 'cleaner' for The Syndicate. He was the man they sent in to clean up messes. Whether it was helping operatives escape from foreign prisons before they made any deals with the authorities compromising The Syndicate, getting rid of an inconvenient dead body, or convincing a loose-tongued buyer that it was in his best interests to keep quiet about who his supplier was, Paine was the man they turned to.

The job that had burned him, the Raj Pink diamond, wasn't even in his wheelhouse. He'd been in the country on another job, for a museum that had hired him to steal back a Klimt. That was how fucked up and incestuous the art world could get. A museum hiring a known art thief to steal back a painting stolen from them. It happened all the time. The museum would arrange a big splashy press release congratulating the authorities for the recovery. The authorities, happy for the good publicity, wouldn't give a damn they'd had nothing to do with it. The insurance company would get their money back and everyone walked away happy.

Which was how he'd been in the country when the auction for the Raj Pink diamond was announced. The diamond had only been found a few years ago and no one expected the Saudi Arabian prince who owned it to let his precious stone go so quickly. There were rumors of insanely high gambling debts as the cause. Since the auction was supposed to be quick and quiet, The Syndicate needed to move fast. He was in the neighborhood, as they say, so he got the call. Except when he'd shown up, someone had beaten him to it. Not too surprising; it wasn't as if he was the only thief eying the stone. What was surprising was when he heard *he* was apparently the one hocking that same stone on the dark web. Someone had set him up. Everything spiraled downward quickly after that job.

The setup was subtle. Clever. Slowly chipping away at his reputation till there was nothing left. The final blow was that fucking Vermeer. He had to admit it was a stroke of genius. Returning a fraud to the museum he had stolen the original from…. Brilliant. It was public so The Syndicate could not help but notice, even though it wasn't a job he'd completed for them. It made a very influential buyer not only drop him but encourage others to do so too. In his line of work, relationships took a long time to build but only seconds to destroy. It only took a whisper of the law being on your back or the inference your stolen goods were not genuine. That was the final straw.

No matter where he'd searched, no matter who he'd questioned with his special interrogation skills, no one knew anything.

The answer was always the same…who the fuck would be stupid enough to cross him?

He'd never had even a hint of suspicion it could be Mira. Mirage as she was referred to in their circles.

Her skills as a thief were legendary. Jewels and sensitive data swiped from corporate computers were her specialty. Given her diminutive, feline physique, it made sense. Paintings, antique sculptures and gold bars, his specialty, were all heavy as hell and usually required a crew for the heist. He excelled not only in the theft but in keeping a wayward crew of criminals in line and under his thumb.

Everyone knew Mirage preferred to work alone. She liked to be the one in complete control.

Like her nickname, she could steal into a building and past some of the most sophisticated security, appearing as no more than a quick bend of light, a glimmering flash. Her presence an illusion until the stolen item was discovered gone. She was discrete about her exploits, so there were only rumors, but he was fairly certain that a job in Antwerp had been hers. Over one million in uncut diamonds had vanished out of a secure vault without so much as a wayward hair or fingerprint left behind. There was the heist at the Carlton Hotel in Paris. The day after the American Ambassador's annual Christmas ball, it was discovered the hotel's safe had been emptied of all the guests' valuables. Not so much as a ring reappeared on the black market. Clever girl had probably ripped every diamond and sapphire out of its setting and then patiently sold them, stone by stone.

Mirage was nothing if not patient, a crucial personality trait in a well-planned revenge scheme.

He respected her for her skills, and he wanted her for her beauty. Like the thief he was, Paine appreciated something precious and rare; Mirage was both.

She was simply stunning. Her petite frame matched her gamine, almost other-worldly features. Skin so pale it was almost translucent. Dark, obsidian eyes which contrasted sharply with her silky blonde hair. Her lips dominated her delicate face, appearing almost too large and always painted a crimson red. Many a night he had lain awake dreaming of that mouth, thinking of the stain of her lipstick on his shaft.

He'd had a small taste, though not enough...perhaps never enough...on that one fateful night in Istanbul two years ago. The rebel faction of the military had staged a coup d'état. The Syndicate had pulled him from a job in

Munich and chartered an emergency flight for him into Turkey.

He was tasked with rescuing a valuable asset. Mirage.

They had hired her to steal government documents during the upheaval which could be used to bribe and coerce future officials on both sides of the coup. It didn't matter to The Syndicate who won just as long as they had dirt on them. The situation in the country erupted in violence sooner than anyone had anticipated. She was holed up in a house near the front lines of the fighting.

At that time, he had known her through reputation alone. As she preferred to work alone, they had never been on a crew or job together. Thieves of their distinction were a rare commodity. It was unusual to not have crossed paths earlier.

He would never forget his first sight of her.

Hiding under a table, she'd been curled up like a frightened kitten. She was dressed much as she was now. All in black. Sleek like a cat. Those beautiful red lips quivering. Her black eyes large and bright with fear. A few specks of blood dotting her cheek. Scanning the room, he saw a corpse lying amongst the rubble.

"It wasn't me." The softly uttered yet defiant claim was the first she had spoken since he'd broken through the door. Her voice was smooth and low, a dark honey.

Ripping the tattered cloth from off the table above her, Paine knelt close to her side. Using an edge of the cloth, he wiped the blood from her pale cheek.

"I wouldn't give a damn if it was, Mira."

He could see her eyes assessing him. In this business, no one could be trusted but it was necessary to learn who could at least be relied upon. He could see she was trying to decide if he was savior or executioner.

"That's not my name," she said finally. "Everyone calls me Mirage."

"I'm not everyone." His lips quirked up in an arrogant smile. "And I'm here to help you. The Syndicate sent me. So you can put down that steak knife you're clutching."

Lowering her eyes and turning her chin slightly away, she didn't even question how he knew her concealed left hand was fisting a knife. He heard the soft thud on the floor as she dropped it. Whether it was because she believed he meant her no harm or that she knew a mere knife would do nothing to stop him from killing her, he couldn't have said.

Turning back to face him, she countered, "Who says I need help?"

Paine knew in that moment she would be his. She immediately fascinated him. Small and vulnerable yet feisty with balls to the wall courage. He wanted to both protect her and push her limits. Not one to waste time, it wasn't long before he'd lifted her slight frame into his arms, ignoring her initial struggles and protestations, and carried her to the first bedroom he could find. Tossing aside the rubble-covered blanket, he pinned her body beneath his own. Never in his life had he wanted to feel the hot grip of a woman's pussy around his cock as much he did in that moment.

And Mira did not disappoint.

He felt like a phoenix, burnt to cinders from her touch, only to be reborn.

The next morning, he had left to do some reconnaissance to figure out the best way to smuggle her out of the country since the military had confiscated the private plane he'd flown in on and closed the airport. When he'd returned, she was gone. Vanished into thin air. As if the entire night had been nothing more than an illusion.

He never did learn how she'd been able to save herself. The Syndicate would only inform him that both of their jobs had been completed. Nothing more. For months, he wasn't even sure if she was alive. Then he learned she had hooked up with that lying sack of shit, Dev. A woman of her beauty, intelligence and skill...of her fire...with that asshole?

Paine wasn't the least bit sorry he'd put a bullet in the piece of shit's head.

Shaking off the past, he tilted his head to look at Mira. Her eyes were closed. Those beautiful, full lips of hers were swollen. The skin along her cheek stained a slight pink from where he had smeared her crimson lipstick with his kiss. A pale streak of light from the coming dawn peeked from between the curtains. The golden light fell on her back. It made her skin glow a rosy pink and showed the faint outline of his fingerprints on her hips from where he had gripped her.

He had taken her on the floor like an animal, like a man possessed.

Between laying eyes on her, the woman who had haunted him for two full years, and her trying to kill him...fury and lust had twisted and turned inside him, battling for control.

Then he'd seen the Raj Pink diamond nestled between her breasts...and he knew.

Knew she was the one who had burned him. Who had ruined his life with her lies, her deceit.

He just still didn't know why.

Rising, he towered over her still, prone form. She hadn't moved or spoken.

He broke the silence. "I want answers, Mira, and you're going to give them to me."

He turned, and despite the early hour, poured himself a whiskey from the sideboard.

Fuck, he needed a drink.

All he heard was a whisper of shifting air.

When he turned back, she was gone. Her still form nothing but an illusion. His little kitten had been primed to run the moment she got a chance.

Dropping his glass, he was at the front door before it could shatter on the hard floor.

It was still locked and secure.

He vaulted up the stairs, turning left into the second bedroom. He knew that was how she'd gained entrance but there was nothing, no hint of movement.

He searched every shadow and dark corner of the tiny safe house but she was nowhere to be found. As in Istanbul, she had vanished into thin air.

Returning downstairs, Paine poured himself another drink, a begrudging smile on his lips. Damn, the woman was good…but he was better.

He would search for her again…and this time he would not give up so easily.

He would find his bad little kitten and make her pay for all her misdeeds.

* * *

"Holy shit, she really did a number on you."

"Shut the fuck up."

Paine was Skyping with Logan, a fellow associate who was currently lying low in Montreal.

Holding an ice pack up to his bruised jaw, Paine grimaced. "A well-placed kick is all."

"And she got a shot off?" Logan gave a low whistle. "Looks like you're slipping, old boy."

"Obviously I let her get that far. I wanted to see who the fuck was out to burn me. I just didn't expect it to be—"

"A woman you fucked one night and left the next morning a couple of years ago…yeah…what are the odds," deadpanned Logan.

"It wasn't like…you know what, fuck you. Do you have a lead on where she might go or not?"

Although preferring to work alone on a per contract basis, Logan was still in The Syndicate's good graces and one of the few who'd never believed the rumors and lies about him. Paine wouldn't say he trusted the guy, but he came as close to it as someone like him ever did.

"Well, there's talk she'll be in London. There is a special exhibit of the Duchess of Devonshire's jewels going up at the Tate in two weeks. The Syndicate has a buyer lined up for two of the diamond necklaces and a pearl bracelet."

Changing the subject, he asked, "Have you tracked down the ex-girlfriend of that idiot who pissed off the cartel yet?" Despite being blacklisted, Paine still had his sources.

Logan just smiled, neither confirming nor denying he had taken the contract to track down some chick named Chloe who had information that just about every nasty character and several governments wanted to get their hands on.

After a moment, Logan turned serious. "Listen, you might want to have a care. If The Syndicate catches wind of this little personal feud you have going on with Mirage, they just might decide to eliminate you both to avoid any possible...unpleasantness."

The Syndicate was a rich-beyond-measure organization of criminals, politicians and businessmen. A blend of the Knights Templar, the Skull and Bones society and some evil Bond villains. They had bankrolled some of the largest heists in the 21st century. Their influence toppled governments and created kings. While it was extremely lucrative to work for them, it was equally dangerous to cross them and they usually acted swiftly at the smallest threat to their organization. Despite his years of working jobs for them, Paine still didn't know a single name or even where they based their operation. They were that cloaked in secrecy. Art and jewelry theft were only a fraction of the shit they were involved in. He suspected it might go as deep as gun trafficking and drugs, but he wasn't sure. All he knew was that they were extremely rich and very powerful. Titan makers and breakers. Only the best got on their payroll. It was a testament to Paine's skills that they had stayed their hand in having him killed so far. Paine wasn't fooled into thinking it was a form of loyalty. They probably needed him for something in the future and could then just as easily kill him later.

"What did she try to kill you with?" asked Logan curiously.

Paine's lips tightened into a thin line. "A .22," he barely uttered.

Logan burst out laughing. "She tried to kill the legendary Paine Darwin with a fucking... .22? I don't know whether she is stupid or fucking insane."

Paine's eyes narrowed. "Careful. That's my woman you're talking about."

Undeterred by his warning, Logan responded sarcastically, "Does she know that?"

"She will when I'm done with her," growled Paine.

"Still…a .22…she might as well have said you have a tiny dick!" Logan laughed.

The rest of his laughter was cut off when Paine abruptly ended the call.

He had a trip to London to plan.

CHAPTER 4

wo weeks later

MIRAGE WALKED BRISKLY into the bright exhibit room. She only spared a quick glance for the empty glass cases with their small black velvet pedestals, primed and ready for the precious diamonds, sapphires and pearls that would soon grace them. Heading for the security guard standing in the corner, she said, "Joe, Mr. Winchester wants to see you. I think he's going to ask about that schedule change you requested."

"Thanks, Josie. I'll tell Martha to watch both rooms and then head on up."

Mirage waited till the security guard had left the space before getting out her phone and quickly snapping several perimeter photos of the room, careful to make sure she recorded the placement of any last-minute additional cameras. It had been a while since she had swiped something from the Tate and this particular exhibit would have more than the usual security.

Museums were understandably very squirrelly about getting background checks on, and fingerprinting, those they hired to be security guards but less so when they hired the secretarial assistant to the head of security. Mirage had lucked out, really. Usually in preparing for heists she had to take a job as a janitor, patiently spending her days dusting display cases and emptying wastepaper baskets as she cased the place. It would normally take weeks for custodial staff to gain access to a special exhibit. As the secretary to the head of security, she was given free rein around the entire museum. Mirage was certain The Syndicate had arranged for the previous secretary to suddenly want to seek new employment, but she never questioned their methods. Too many questions always led to trouble in her opinion.

These final photos were all she needed to complete her reconnaissance. She knew the security schedule, the floor plan of the exhibit, the placement of the cameras and lasers and her exit route. The new exhibit of the Duchess of Devonshire's jewels opened tomorrow. They would be placing the jewels in their display cases tonight after the museum closed to the public. She would need to strike tonight after the staff had gone. All that was left to do was grab the two GoPro cameras she had staged a few days ago by the security keypads and collect the data on the proper passwords and she would be all set.

It was not ideal. She would have preferred to wait. To

watch the exhibit and its patterns a little longer, but there was no time. She needed to keep moving from job to job, country to country if she wanted to stay out of the reach of *him*. The key was to focus, she reminded herself. *And not think of Paine*, said the evil voice in her head. She hadn't had a moment of peace since that night in D.C. Every night in bed, she replayed in her head what had happened. How she'd let it get so out of hand. How her body had responded. She couldn't understand the man's influence over her. She barely knew him for fuck's sake. Yet with a single touch he had managed to derail months of careful planning. Made her forget all about Dev, about revenge, about killing him. Mirage gritted her teeth at the thought of it.

Her opportunity was lost.

Paine now knew it was she who had set him up.

For two weeks, she had barely slept. Jumping at every noise, checking under her bed and in closets for the monster she knew was lurking there. She knew he would come for her.

She'd had her chance at revenge.

It was now his turn.

For some reason, she knew he wouldn't tell The Syndicate what she had done. Her life wouldn't be worth shit if he did. No, this was personal and they both knew it. He was the type of man who would handle his own problems.

Reaching into her collar, her fingers skimmed down the metal chain around her neck till they touched the smooth, warm surface of the pink diamond. It was the height of insanity to keep it. She should have tried to fence it, or better yet, thrown it into the Potomac River the moment she'd gotten away from Paine. It was the only thing that could truly connect her to Paine's thwarted theft of it. A tangible reminder of her deception and guilt in the matter.

But there was a much greater guilt weighing on her, thought Mirage. The kill contract she had just taken out on Paine Darwin.

This was no longer about revenge but survival.

She had no choice in the matter. Now that he knew it was her, he would be coming after her for certain.

What a fucking mess she had created! If she didn't put the contract out on Paine, he would find her and kill her. By putting the contract out on him, she was basically waving a red flag in front of The Syndicate. It would only be a matter of time before they figured out she was the one who'd stolen the Raj Pink diamond, who'd fabricated the Vermeer story, and who'd taken one of their best men out of the field with her lies and deception. What had made her think she could just ruin Paine's life, kill him, and walk away with no consequences? In avenging Dev's death, she may have just ruined her own.

You make your choices. Life will choose your consequences, as her grandfather used to always remind her.

Control. Control over your actions and reactions was the only way to avoid the type of consequences that usually befell her type—criminals. She had forgotten those lessons. She'd let her emotions get the better of her and allowed her reactions to control her rather than the other way around.

What a fucking mess, she thought again for the thousandth time.

Well, she needed this final score and then she would be in the wind. Mirage would truly become an illusion, a memory. She would cease to exist. Disappear.

It was the only way. Still, she couldn't shake the guilt.

The irony that she was suddenly feeling guilty about putting out a contract to kill a man she herself had tried to kill just a few weeks ago was not lost on her. Things had suddenly shifted. Changed. Her revenge schemes were fine until she was standing over his bed with a gun. Suddenly it was no longer a game, a fantasy she had worked out in her head. It was real with tangible consequences. It was easier when she just burned him from afar. She could separate herself, keep telling herself it was justified, deserved. But facing off with the man himself, seeing the anger in his eyes, and sensing his hurt and confusion about her betrayal… Mirage shivered, suddenly feeling chilled.

Yes, it was the height of insanity to keep the pink diamond.

Mirage tucked the stone and chain safely back inside her shirt and turned to leave the exhibit.

She never saw the tall man angrily observing her every move.

* * *

Keeping to the shadows, she walked along Castle Yard Road, preferring never to drive up to a target. Making her way to the back of the building, careful to avoid the reach of the perimeter cameras, Mirage knelt before a large silver panel marked 'Danger, High Voltage Electrical Equipment.' Using her pneumatic flush cutters, she severed the hinges to the panel. She then silently removed the screws. Placing the panel to the side, she surveyed the aluminum grating covering a four-foot duct. It was only secured with a simple padlock. Reaching blindly behind her, Mirage felt for the cutters she had laid aside.

A large warm hand clasped her wrist.

Too well-trained to call out, she turned and glared at Paine. Her clenched teeth stifled a hiss of anger.

Laying a finger to his lips, he then pointed to the left.

Mirage watched as a single black Mercedes-Benz S550 slowly wound its way down a small alley toward the Tate. No doubt it was the armored version with bulletproof glass, a steel cage protecting the fuel tank and battery, and flat-proof tires.

Germans, mouthed Paine.

Mirage nodded.

There was a German crew who often tried to hit the same targets. They were extremely well-funded by an organization which competed with The Syndicate for dominance and didn't mind a little blood splatter on the artwork.

Dammit, thought Mirage. She'd known in her gut tonight was the wrong night. Her impatience had almost gotten her busted or killed.

Paine dragged her by the arm, keeping to the shadows. They moved at a swift pace till they reached Shakespeare's Globe. He had a car parked on the other side.

It was then Mirage found her voice. Pulling on her

arm, she dug in her feet. "I'm not getting in a car with you!"

"You have no choice in the matter."

"The hell I don't. If you don't let go, I'll scream."

Paine leaned in close. She could smell the spicy scent of his aftershave. "Go ahead and scream, kitten," he boldly dared.

Mirage's lips thinned. He knew she would never alert the police to their whereabouts. Too many questions would be asked. Too many questions led to trouble.

More afraid than she had ever been in her life, she begged, "Just let me go. I'll disappear. You will never lay eyes on me again."

Paine smirked. "That's what I'm afraid of. Now are you going to get into the car like a good girl or do I have to go to Plan B?"

Mirage stubbornly crossed her arms and glared at him.

Two seconds later, she was pounding on the inside roof of his trunk cursing him to hell and back.

* * *

SHE WAS STUCK in that trunk for at least twenty minutes. Judging by the smooth ride, he must have taken her to the outer limits of London where it was less populated. The moment the car stopped, Mirage prepared herself. When the trunk lid swung open, she kicked out with both feet before agilely jumping out of the trunk. She had barely started to run before there was a hand grabbing the back of her shirt.

"I swear to God, I'm going to put a leash on you if you don't stop running away from me, babygirl."

Her sarcastic retort was cut off as he put a shoulder to her stomach and lifted her into the air, carrying her into a remote house on the outskirts of London. She only caught glimpses of a red brick façade outside and a shabby living room with worn furniture inside before he carried her into a small, well-lit bedroom and deposited her onto the bed. Before she had even bounced up, she was on her feet, squaring off with him.

Mirage realized with a start it was the first time she had seen him in full light. He seemed even taller and more imposing. Like her, he was dressed in unrelenting black. The strong angles of his jaw, brow and cheekbones gave him an almost sinister quality. His eyes were so light they were almost a crystalline blue. Stubble dusted his cheeks as if he hadn't shaved in weeks. His wavy brown hair looked ruffled and unkempt. In short, he looked like a man who had been on the hunt.

Mirage turned her head right then left, looking for an escape route.

"There is none," he intoned as she watched him uncoil a length of black nylon rope that had been resting on a nearby chair.

"It's time you and I had a little chat. You're going to tell me why you tried to kill me and why you burned me."

"Go to hell," she spat.

"Oh, I've had my ticket punched for that trip for a long time," Paine said with a seductive wink.

"You know why," she said through gritted teeth. "Don't insult me by pretending you don't."

"I assure you I don't. Although I must confess, whatever it is…I can't honestly say I regret it. Not if it inspired such beautiful anger in those dark eyes of yours. There really is nothing quite as stimulating as a hate fuck."

With a shrill scream of indignation, Mirage launched herself at him, claws bared. Paine took a step back before quickly looping a simple slip knot over both her wrists and pulling tight. Still she tried to fight him. Dragging her by the rope, he pushed her onto the bed and secured the rope to the headboard, her arms stretched tight over her head.

"I have some questions for you, baby. And you have a rather annoying habit of disappearing on me or trying to kill me. I think this little arrangement will help prevent that, don't you?"

"You fucking bastard. Let me go! I'll kill you for this!" she screeched as she swung her legs out trying to kick him.

"You already tried and missed, and I'm sure you remember your punishment for it."

Mirage's cheeks heated at the illicit memory. How he'd fucked her from behind, both of them lost in a primal dance of lust and loathing.

Still she would get a little of her own back.

A smug light came into her eyes. "Yes, but the man I hired won't."

She shouldn't have told him. Should have kept her mouth shut, but something about this man made her want to push his buttons . To court danger. It was an adrenaline rush watching the anger spark in his eyes, his jaw tighten, his fists clench. She loved knowing she had done that, had broken the famous icy reserve of Paine Darwin. All her careful control snapped when she was in his presence. She became reckless, foolish, glorying in the dangerous thrill of poking a ferocious beast with a stick.

Paine grabbed her around the throat. His large fist squeezed. "You put a fucking hit out on me?"

Mirage closed her eyes and focused on breathing through her nose.

"Answer me, dammit. Who? When?"

She opened her eyes and stared defiantly back at him.

The bed dipped as he rested one knee on it. Keeping his grip on her throat, he leaned down to whisper, "I think it is past time you learned why they call me Paine."

Her eyes widened when she saw the knife in his hand. Mirage stilled.

You make your choices. Life will choose your consequences.

She could feel the tip of the knife move down the exposed column of her throat. There was a gentle tug on the neckline of her T-shirt then the sound of fabric rending. He had cut her T-shirt open. Worse, she was completely bare underneath. A bra hindered movement when she was working.

Paine finished slicing off her shirt then lifted the chain which held the pink diamond with his blade. Cocking one knowing eyebrow at her, he flicked his wrist and broke the chain, catching the falling diamond in his fist and pocketing it.

Mirage held her breath when she then felt the tip of the knife circle one erect nipple.

"You have the most gorgeous breasts. Did you know that, Mira? In both of our brief encounters, I didn't have the time to truly appreciate your curves. I plan to rectify that now." His voice was dark and low.

He placed the edge of the knife between her breasts and moved it downward.

Dismayed, Mirage looked down. She could see a faint pink line against her pale skin but no blood. Yet.

Using two fingers, he tugged on the waistband of her yoga pants. Pulling them away from her stomach, he gave her another wink as if this was all just some game before slicing into the thin fabric with his knife. Down one leg, then the other. She was naked before his prying eyes.

"I hate you," she hissed as tears filled her eyes.

He ran a knuckle down her cheek. "That is a shame, kitten, because you fascinate me." He leaned in close to breathe against her open mouth, "And I don't think you hate me nearly as much as you say you do."

Mirage turned her head away, trying again to pull on the binds securing her wrists. She could hear him take off his shirt and kick off his shoes. She stubbornly kept her head averted.

She only turned her gaze back to him when she heard him unbuckle his belt.

Her inner thighs clenched tight. Her whole body trembled.

Jesus Christ, what the fuck was wrong with her? This was depraved, wrong.

Had her life become so fucked up? So twisted? So on the dark side that something like this turned her on? Had she slipped so far from normal that only the adrenaline rush that came from pain and the fear of death could make her pulse race? The truth burned like a brand. It had been true in Istanbul. It had been true when she'd broken into his home and it was true now. To her utter damnation, he fascinated her too. She kept her life and emotions ruthlessly in control. Was patient, careful, organized.

When she was with him, nothing was in her control. He dominated everything. Her thoughts. Her body. Everything. She felt as if she were constantly spinning, the world tilting and whirling by. Like a true thief, he didn't ask…he just took what he wanted. There was something undeniably arousing about a man like that.

Dev had made her feel important. Always asking her opinion on heists, encouraging her to challenge herself and take jobs she thought were too difficult. Offering to fence the jewels so she could focus on the next job.

The hard truth was Paine made her feel like…like…all that was decent, kind and secure, all that made people civilized, all that kept the baser impulses in check, had been stripped away. Leaving only what was raw, primal and true. It was an experience she had begun to crave. A high like no other. The extremes of all conflicting emotions colliding in a starburst of light. Pain, pleasure, hate…love. It explained why she only needed to be around him to react to his powerful presence. They did not have to go through the polite niceties of casual dates of dinners and movies, or long conversations on the phone getting to know one another.

This was more elemental. Base. Animalistic.

Still she fought.

Mirage didn't like this feeling of spinning out of

control. Didn't want his dominance. He and it frightened her.

She watched in horrified fascination as he looped his thick leather belt in half and slapped it against one large palm.

"Time for your punishment, babygirl."

CHAPTER 5

*H*e must be out of his goddamned fucking mind, thought Paine.

This woman was poison. A cocked gun at his head. A noose around his throat.

She not only was going to get him killed, she had put out the fucking hit to make it happen! Yet all he could think about was bending her to his will. She was so defiant, so stubborn, so fucking smart and beautiful. She both fascinated and excited him. Never in his life had he met a woman who challenged him like Mirage.

He wanted, no needed, to hear her beg.

With his free hand, he flipped her onto her stomach.

Her tawny hair hung in waves over her shoulders and partially down her back. He loved the slope of her back, how it dipped low then crested over the generous curve of her ass.

Raising his arm high, he brought the heavy belt down on that beautiful ass like a lash.

Her scream was muffled by the pillow.

Her pale, creamy skin burst into a bright cherry pink line straight across both cheeks. His cock lengthened at the sight. He raised his arm again, this time striking her across the tops of her thighs.

"Stop! Stop!"

It was not enough. He lashed her again, then again with his belt. Her ass glowed a beautiful crimson red. Unable to resist, he cupped her left bottom cheek, needing to feel the heat radiating off her skin, knowing it was glowing from his punishment, his mark.

Her legs kicked the bed as her fingers clenched on the headboard.

"Oh God! It hurts!"

Bringing the belt down one last time across her cheeks, he watched as they bounced and jiggled from the strike. Turning white for just a moment before bursting into a deep flush.

Unable to stand it any longer, he tore at the fastening of his jeans.

Freeing his cock, he kicked the pants aside and knelt on the bed. He positioned himself between her legs. Placing his hands on her hips, he raised her up onto her knees. Running two fingers over her cunt, he could feel her slick heat. She could cry and scream all she wanted.

She may hate him, but she still wanted him.

Fisting his thick shaft, his voice was harsh with need. "Beg me to fuck you. I want to hear you say it again."

Memories of her deep-throated moans when he'd forced her to come as he spanked her ass while his cock was buried deep in her cunt still haunted his dreams. It had become an obsession.

"Go to hell."

He slapped her already reddened ass. Her head raised up and back as she moaned from either pain or pleasure; he couldn't tell and didn't care.

"Beg me to fuck your cunt."

"No," she rasped defiantly.

Paine shook his head. His beautifully stubborn little kitten always had to learn the hard way, he supposed. "Have it your way."

Placing the head of his cock between her legs, he shifted his hips, rubbing her pussy, teasing her.

When the tip was wet from her dew, he brushed it against her asshole. The tiny pink puckered skin protecting her forbidden entrance clenched and stiffened.

"No! No! No! Don't you dare fuck me in the ass, Paine."

He pushed on her entrance with the head of his cock, watching the pale pink skin whiten from the pressure as it glistened from her own arousal.

Her hips bucked, trying to dislodge him. He spanked her ass again.

The momentary pain stilled her.

He thrust harder, needing to push past her resisting band of muscle. Thrusting forward with his hips while pulling back on her own, the head of his shaft pushed inside.

Mirage gave out a howl of pain.

"No! It hurts! Take it out! Take it out!"

He drove his hips forward, forcing her body to accept several inches of his thick shaft up her ass.

"Where is my cock, Mira? Where is it?" he shouted.

"It's in my ass," she cried.

He pulled back before thrusting forward again, deeper…harder.

"Ow! Ow! Oh, God!"

She had taken about five inches. She still had another five to accept. Paine felt a rush of primal possession as he leaned into her body, forcing her to submit to his greater strength. Bending her to his will. Hearing her moan with pleasure-tinged pain. Compelling her to beg, to accept his dominance.

"Why is my cock in your ass?" he growled, scraping the sharp edge of his teeth along the soft slope of her shoulder.

"I don't know," she whined.

"Because you were a bad girl."

He could feel her body tighten and clutch at his cock. She was so goddamn tight.

"Say it," he ground out. "Say you were a bad girl."

"Bite me," she spit out through gritted teeth.

The edge of his teeth along her shoulder blades answered her taunt.

"I wouldn't keep me waiting if I were you, baby. I can always make this more painful. Now say it."

There was a long pause.

He pushed in to the hilt. Her ass had taken the full ten inches. He could see her body strain to accept him. A bright sheen of sweat glimmered on her lower back. She yelled in agony the moment his balls hit the underside of her ass.

Finally, she obeyed. "I was a bad girl. I was a bad girl. Please, stop."

Shifting his right hand from her hip, he reached between her legs. Finding her sensitive nub, he flicked it with two fingers before rubbing it in small circles, slowly building the pressure.

Mirage moaned.

He leaned down and bit her shoulder, as a stallion would his mare while mating. Licking the spot he'd marked, tasting her skin, he demanded, "Say you want this. Say you like the pain."

'Please!" she moaned. The deep-throated kind that only came from pleasure.

"Admit it," he growled. "You like when I force you. You like the feel of my cock filling your ass. You like submitting to me. Need it."

Her back arched as her hips pushed back the moment his two fingers thrust inside her wet pussy.

Moving his left hand, he grabbed her hair, ruthlessly pulling her head back by the cascading tresses.

"Say it," he ordered.

"I like the pain," she cried.

"Beg me to fuck you harder. Beg me to make it hurt," he rasped against her neck.

"Please, Paine. Make it hurt! Fuck me!"

At her admission, the sound of his name on her lips, his balls tightened as a surge of pleasurable pressure hit his cock. Fisting her hair, he leaned back and began to savagely slam his cock into her body.

Mirage screamed. Angry red marks appeared around the binds on her wrists as her knuckles whitened from her straining grip on the headboard.

His mind went blank. Every sense was focused on the

feel of her leather-warmed skin as it brushed against his hips. How her body firmly gripped his cock. The silken feel of her hair in his palm. The sound of her harsh breathing as she moaned.

His cock so tightly filled her back passage he could feel the ripples of her own orgasm as it crested over her. Mirage cried out before falling limp. He thrust again. This time he wanted to mark her both inside and out. Refusing to pull out, when he came, it was deep inside her ass.

* * *

He held a glass of red wine to her lips. Mirage took a grateful sip, uncaring as the ruby liquid dribbled down her chin and onto her naked breast.

Paine leaned over and laved at her skin, taking her nipple between his lips as he sucked the wine droplet up.

Mirage gasped at the intimacy of the act. Anyone would have thought they were newlyweds tucked away in a quaint cottage for their honeymoon. But they weren't newlyweds. Scenes like that were for normal people. Paine and she would never be normal. There was a twinge of guilt as she remembered how close she had come to normal once. How desperately she had reached out for that kind of life, but now it was all gone.

Taking a sip himself, he put the glass aside and tilted up her chin. Still tied to the bed, she was sitting with her legs tucked up to the side. Her wrists raised before her, almost as if in prayer.

"No more games, Mira. Tell me."

She looked into his ice blue eyes. The utter ridiculousness of her situation hit her. She was tied up naked in Paine's bed. He'd just fucked her ass. *Her ass.* And she'd begged him to do it harder. All while wanting this man dead for killing the man she'd supposedly loved who she now realized didn't come close to rocking her to her core as Paine had just done.

Mirage tilted her head forward. Her shoulders started to shake.

"Baby?" asked Paine as he tried to push her soft hair out of the way so he could see her face.

Mirage could hear the concern in his voice and her shoulders shook harder.

He finally realized she was laughing.

"I'd love to join in on the joke, Mira."

She sucked in a choking breath. "You're making me crazy, you know that? I don't know my own mind anymore. I hate you! I really do." There was no mirth to her laughter. It was almost maniacal, unhinged.

"I think the bullet fired into my pillow established that," he drawled.

Mirage sobered.

Composing herself, she said, "You killed Dev."

She watched him as he took in her words. A look of utter disbelief crossed his stern features. "That's what this is about? That piece of shit, Doug?"

Mirage shook her head. "No. Not Doug. Dev. You killed Dev."

"I know who I killed, Mira. His name was Doug."

Her brow wrinkled. Wait, she had always assumed Dev was short for Devon. How could she be in love with a man and not know his real name? Of course, she had never told him her real name either.

"So you don't deny it?"

"Why would I? The guy was an asshole. He more than deserved what he got."

"I loved him."

"No you didn't."

"Don't say that! You don't know. You don't know anything about me!" she yelled.

"I know you are a beautiful, vivacious, stubborn, feisty woman who makes a man want to strangle you and kiss you at the same time. I know you feel things deeply and completely. I know you try so hard to keep a tight rein on every aspect of your life that when something forces you to let go, it is like watching the birth of a star. You are all light and color and energy when you come, baby. Someone like that couldn't possibly truly be in love with a shallow, lying piece of shit like Devious Doug. He used you. Everyone knew. Even The Syndicate. All those hand-picked jobs. How he pushed you into dangerous situations for more and more money. It was all a lie, baby. He was using you. Only telling you what you wanted to hear."

Tears coursed down her cheeks at his words. The truth of it. She realized now she had so desperately just wanted to experience something normal like falling in love. Something common and domestic and boring. She had wanted to be in love with a boyfriend. She had wanted it so badly, that fantasy of normal, that she had overlooked all the flags and warnings. How she was getting less and less money for the items he fenced. The unexplained absences. When that dream of normalcy was taken away, she'd reverted back to her dark, underworld training. Revenge was her only thought. Her only focus. In her grief, she had turned Dev's memory into some idealized version of him. Magnified her love for him to the point of obsession to avenge his death by going after his killer. Still, she needed to know. Closure was an illusion, but perhaps she could get some answers.

"Why? Why did you kill him?"

Paine shrugged his shoulders. "The Syndicate ordered it."

Mirage watched him intently. There was something he wasn't telling her. "What is it? Tell me."

Before telling her, Paine grabbed the crumpled blanket from the bed and placed it over her shoulders.

It was a kind, caring gesture, and Mirage resented the hell out of it.

He was shattering her world, but worse…he was pitying her for it. She didn't want anyone's pity, least of all his. Especially not for being a fool. Falling for the lies of some asshole because he called her pretty and said he wanted to be her boyfriend? How stupid could she be?

"Tell me," she repeated.

"He was getting involved in the sex traffic trade. That is one line even The Syndicate will not cross. It threatened their interests. So they ordered him killed."

"Why you? Why did it have to be you? I mean I know…your name…and reputation but you're mainly a thief for them not an assassin."

His jaw tightened and his lips thinned. "I've answered enough questions. Tell me about the hit."

Mirage cringed. "I thought you were going to kill me after…after…I didn't…I'm still not sure you—"

"Tell me about the hit, Mira."

"The contract was accepted five hours ago," she whispered.

"Who?"

"Pearly."

Ted "Pearly" Gates was one of the best in the business. He was clean, efficient and more importantly…fast. Once he accepted a contract, it was usually only twenty-four hours before it was completed.

Grabbing the wine glass, Paine drained it as he turned his back on her for a moment. Turning back around, he said, "Pearly accepted a hit against me? Me? I've played poker with that backstabbing dick."

Mirage shrugged her shoulders. "He said if he didn't do it, someone else would. Plus I…I offered him the…the Jubilee."

"I fucking knew that heist was you!" said Paine as he pointed at her.

The Jubilee was a seventy-eight-carat uncut diamond found in Russia. The seller had announced it was to be put on the market, but it had disappeared from a highly secured Geneva bank before the auction could take place. It had been a theft of pure mastery. His first thought at the time was it had to be his girl, Mira. *Even then he'd thought of her as his.*

Sending him a shy smile, Mirage just nodded her head. She had kept that particular heist a secret from everyone. Even Dev. In retrospect, her instincts were probably telling her something was wrong even back then. She'd just refused to listen to them.

"Well, I guess if a friend is going to betray you, it might as well be for a diamond worth tens of millions."

Paine reached for her. Mirage flinched as she craned her body back as far as the binds would allow.

"Are you going to kill me now?"

"No, my reckless little fool. We need to go find Pearly and clean up your mess."

CHAPTER 6

"Absolutely not."

"I'm sorry. Did I start that sentence with 'if it pleases Her Majesty'?" came his angry retort.

"I am not riding about the countryside with a man who has a contract out on his head!"

Paine curled his hands into fists as if to keep from strangling her. "It's because of *you* I *have* that contract on my head."

Mirage tossed her head, her tawny waves falling over her shoulders. "Moot point. Besides, I'm not entirely convinced you're still not going to try to kill me."

Paine grabbed her by the chin. His eyes flashed an icy blue. "At this very moment, neither am I, kitten." He placed a hard kiss on her lips before turning away.

"Will you at least untie me and give me some clothes?"

His only response was a bark of laughter over his shoulder as he left the bedroom.

* * *

A HALF HOUR later she was bundled up in a blanket, naked as jaybird underneath, in the passenger seat of his car. Since she'd been told in no uncertain terms she could just as easily be riding in the trunk, Mirage was making the best of it.

"I'm staying at the Dorchester in Mayfair."

"How nice for you," he responded as he directed the car in the opposite direction.

"Hey! You are seriously not going to take me back to my hotel so I can get some clothes?"

"Nope."

"I don't have any money or ID or my phone," she complained. She never carried anything that could possibly identify her when working on a job. She even hid her room key somewhere outside the hotel to await her return since she knew they could also be tracked.

Paine gave her a once-over, then a quick wink. "I figure that should slow your escape down to at least half speed. If Pearly is going to call off the hit, I need you by my side to do it, and you have a nasty little habit of disappearing on me. I still haven't figured out how the fuck you managed to get out of that safe house in D.C. so quickly without going through the bedroom window or the front door." His voice held a hint of pride mixed with appreciation.

Mirage only half hid her smile.

"What can I say? I'm a natural," came her saucy response.

It wasn't hard to be a natural when your grandfather had taught you how to break into a home from the time you were six years old. It wasn't his fault. He hadn't been a bad man. Hell, he hadn't even been a criminal until after… after…that night. The night her parents were killed in a car accident. As a retired steel worker, he hadn't had the money to support a little girl and was desperate to not have the State take her away. So, he'd done what he had to do to keep her. He'd done it out of love. He'd even made most of it into a game. And it was fun, until he'd gotten arrested when she was seventeen. Her beloved grandfather had died in prison. She'd been left alone. A life of crime was all she had ever known. The only stable thing in her life, as odd as that seemed. There'd been no turning back at that point. She'd decided from that moment forward she would be the best there was. She would plan and do each heist with precision. Control. Control. Control. It was how she lived her life. No risks. No unknowns. Everything planned and researched.

Her attraction to Paine was not a part of the plan.

His ability to seize control of her body and even her mind was not a part of the plan.

Her submissive reaction to the dominance of his touch was definitely not a part of the plan.

And she wouldn't even *think* about the spanking kink being part of the plan.

Nothing was going according to plan, and Mirage was trying very hard not to panic.

She had been a fool to believe Dev had cared and loved her. She would not allow herself to go down that same path with Paine. A man who still very well may kill her.

She had to get control back.

She had to escape.

* * *

"Here you go," said Paine as he tossed a white plastic shopping bag onto her lap.

Mirage opened the bag. Closing it with a huff, she sent him a glare.

"What? You wanted clothes," he said with a smirk.

"Seriously?" said Mirage as she pulled out one of the items and held it up for his inspection.

"I got you a T-shirt and yoga pants. I noticed that's what you like to wear," Paine said, looking for all the world as innocent as a newborn babe.

Mirage's entire wardrobe consisted of black T-shirts and black yoga pants. The only variation was the occasional long-sleeved T-shirt. Despite what was shown on television, fiber evidence was no good to the police if it was a common fiber that could not be traced. There was nothing more common and boring than black T-shirts and yoga pants, except for maybe jeans, but those fibers were traceable. The T-shirt and yoga pants outfit was ideal for heists and quick escapes, and if she were to ever have to leave her luggage behind, her wardrobe would tell the police nothing about her, her travels or her personality. Control. Control. Control. Even her wardrobe was held under rigid control.

Except for now, when she was with Paine.

Mirage held up a bright pink T-shirt with the image of a kitten on it and neon blue yoga pants. "Really?"

"What? The kitten is cute. It's what I think about whenever I look at you. An adorable sleek kitten with a set of nasty claws."

Mirage blushed at the strangely flattering comparison. Shaking off the warm sentiment toward him, she said, "And the blue neon pants? These are atrocious."

Paine gave her a knowing smile. "It's a lot harder to escape into thin air wearing a pair of neon pants. Besides, it will be nice to see some color on you."

Mirage's dark eyes narrowed. "I hate you."

Paine turned his attention back to the road. "So you keep saying," he responded in a teasing sing-song voice.

She continued to dig in the bag. At the bottom was a tube of deep crimson lipstick. She shot Paine a questioning look.

The look of pure sexual possession and promise in his eyes was the only response she needed.

Mirage didn't think her cheeks could blush any hotter.

She was quickly proven wrong when he refused to allow her to go to the ladies' room to change.

"You just want me to change right here in the car?"

"It's nothing I haven't seen before or will again."

Mirage struggled to maneuver the blanket so he didn't see so much as a flash of skin as she put on the clothes, all the while muttering how she hoped Pearly didn't miss his mark.

"What was that?"

"I said we're off to a banging start," Mirage retorted, taking her turn at looking for all the world as innocent as a newborn babe.

* * *

MIRAGE COULD FEEL his warm hand brush her cheek but pretended to be asleep. The car had stopped a few minutes ago. They had been driving for at least three hours. She hadn't bothered to ask him where because she knew he wouldn't tell her. She could feel him unbuckle her seat belt and then gather her into his arms. She rested her head against his shoulder, liking the feel of his soft flannel shirt and the smell of his cologne.

Still, she pretended to be asleep. She didn't want him to know she liked the feel of his arms holding her, or that she felt strangely safe. It reminded her how she'd felt when he'd broken down the barricaded door in Istanbul. With the bright light shining behind him, all she could make out was this tall, imposing figure. She hadn't known if he was the military or the police or any number of other possible enemies. Then he had knelt before her and wiped her cheek and she'd known she was safe and was going to be all right.

Except then she'd run, just as she was planning to do now. Feeling safe and warm, relying on someone, all of those were foreign, frightening emotions for her. Perhaps that was why she'd convinced herself she was in love with Dev. He'd just been someone who was there, who understood her life choices, who didn't judge, who could let her pretend everything was normal. But he wasn't someone who'd made her feel safe or protected. If he had, she would have run from him too.

She was jostled a bit as Paine opened the door to wherever he was taking her. The place was cold with a musty, shut-in smell. Paine placed her gently on something soft but firm. It was probably a sofa she thought, still refusing to open her eyes. She could hear him moving about. There was a scraping sound then the smell of sulfur. Soon she heard the crackle and pop of a fire. The room filled with the scent of pine and burning cedar. Tilting her head back slightly, she could feel the warmth from the flames.

Listening, she could hear sounds coming from the kitchen; the quiet clang of a metal pot hitting the stove, the whoosh sound of cabinets being opened and searched, the clink of a utensil as it was laid against a china plate. If she listened closely, she could even swear she heard Paine humming a soft tune.

It all felt so domestic. So cozy.

So wrong.

They weren't some cute couple in love on a holiday. They were two thieves hiding out from a contract killer whom she'd hired.

Two thieves who hated one another. *Didn't they?*

Mirage threw aside the blanket and rose, taking in her surroundings. They were in a small, rustic cottage with bare stone walls, exposed timber beams and old, blown-glass windows. The furniture was sturdy with a rich, royal blue upholstery. The room had a masculine feel because of the heavy wooden furnishings but with subtle feminine touches. A delicate vase was on the bookshelf. Pictures of wildflowers hung on the walls. Little lace doilies lay on all the small tables' surfaces. The place was adorable. It felt like a home.

It made everything worse.

Mirage marched in the direction of the noises and found him in a tiny kitchen. The windows sent a honey glow of light into the darkness outside. She could see into the small yard with its vegetable garden and little, dilapidated picket fence and beyond to the open rough sea. They must be somewhere along the coast, thought Mirage.

"You're just in time. I made macaroni and cheese... although without the milk, so I can't be held responsible for how it tastes," teased Paine with a wink. "We aren't exactly expected guests here, so the larder wasn't stocked. I did buy some wine when I got your clothes. Corkscrew is in the drawer. Why don't you open the bottle for us?"

He was scooping the clumpy bright orange pasta into two bowls as he spoke. Casually. Calmly. As if he were talking to a date or a girlfriend.

"I'm not hungry, and the last thing I'm going to do is get drunk around you again." The memory of Istanbul was at the front of her mind. She'd gotten drunk on whiskey while the world erupted into chaos around them. Memories of the passionate night that followed had Mirage ruthlessly pushing away the seductive pull of the shadows from the past.

"You'll eat anyway, baby. You haven't eaten all day," he commanded.

"I said I'm not fucking hungry." Mirage pushed the bowl away.

Paine put down the pot and turned to stare at her.

"Careful, kitten. Your claws are showing." He took a step toward her.

"So what if they are, I didn't ask to be brought here!" Mirage took a step backward in spite of her defiant words.

"I'm beginning to believe you antagonize me on purpose, just so I'll fuck you. Baby, if you want my cock, all you have to do is ask."

"You're a bastard and I hate you." Her breath came in excited gasps as her cheeks began to heat, warming up for the fight ahead.

Paine took another step toward her as he reached to unbuckle his belt.

Mirage held out a hand in warning. "Don't you dare!"

Paine whipped the belt free of his jeans' loops. He then held it between his hands, taking several steps toward her as Mirage quickly retreated.

"I think you like this. Crave it. The fight. The chase. The adrenaline rush when I capture you. Force you."

Mirage's eyes sparked with fury, hating the truth of his words. Her nipples tightened as her stomach clenched. She could feel herself getting wet as he silently approached. Still she tried to deny it. "It's not true," she fired back at him.

"How do you want it this time, Mira? I already took that sweet cunt and tight ass of yours. I think this time I want your mouth."

"Oh, God!" she moaned, resisting the urge to close her eyes and let his dark, dangerous words penetrate to her bones.

Paine lunged for her.

Mirage screamed and ran. Unfamiliar with the layout of the house, she ran blindly down one hall, around a corner then into another room. "Fuck!" It was a bedroom, with no exit.

She turned to flee.

Paine was standing in the doorway. He had tossed his shirt aside, exposing a strong muscular chest with thin swirls of black hair. Thick biceps. Wide shoulders. A flat stomach. Mirage devoured every inch with her gaze and hated herself for it.

He stepped into the room as he unzipped his jeans.

Mirage grabbed a small figurine which rested on a bureau and launched it at his head.

He deftly twisted his shoulders. The figure smashed against the wall.

He lunged again.

Grabbing her by the throat, he pressed her back against the wall.

Kissing and nipping at the smooth column of her neck, he worked his way up to her ear. "Brace yourself, kitten. This is going to hurt."

Mirage couldn't breathe. A lightheaded euphoria began to drift over her senses. Finally, he relinquished his grip on her throat only to push her to her knees.

Taking his belt, he wrapped the thick leather around her neck, pushing the end through the heavy buckle and pulling just tight enough to slightly squeeze her throat.

Mirage placed a hand between her legs and rubbed her throbbing cunt.

Paine yanked on the belt. "No touching that pretty little cunt of yours until you've finished sucking my cock."

Her eyes lit with defiance. Just to test him, she closed her lips tight, breathing swiftly through her nose in her rising arousal.

Paine reached down and grasped her cheeks. The tips of his fingers pressed in. The delicate skin inside her mouth cut against the sharp edges of her teeth. With a cry, she relented and opened her mouth.

"Good girl," he growled.

Releasing his grip on her face but keeping hold of the belt, he reached inside his jeans to pull out his thick shaft.

Mirage felt a trickle of fear curl deep within her chest. He was so big. So thick. She had never really liked giving oral, so she had next to no practice. There was no way she was going to be able to satisfy a man like Paine.

"I... don't... I can't...."

"You can and you will. Open your mouth."

Mirage whimpered as the heavy, bulbous head of his cock pushed past her lips.

Her tongue swirled around the tip before he pushed in further. Shifting his hips forward, his shaft slipped unrestricted further into her open mouth. Mirage's chest convulsed as she made a gurgling sound, fighting for breath. Desperately yanking on the restraining belt around her neck, she tried to pull her head back, but it hit the resistance of the wall behind her kneeling form. His cock filled her mouth, the wide shaft pressing down on her tongue, the bulging tip pushing against the back of her throat, cutting off her air.

Paine kept a firm grip on his shaft for another moment before relenting. He pulled free. Mirage fell forward, taking choking gulps of air into her lungs.

Once again he grabbed the belt and forced her head up. Looking down at her tear-streaked cheeks, he warned, "Take a deep breath."

Panicked, she tried to shake her head but couldn't before he drove his cock into her mouth again. Moving his hips back and forth, he pulsed the head of his cock in short thrusts, hitting sensitive nerves at the back of her throat. She gagged but he refused to relent. Just kept thrusting. Using her. Fucking her mouth.

Mirage's jaw ached from trying to keep her lips open around his thrusting cock. The underside of her tongue felt cut from where it pressed against her teeth. The back of her throat was tender and swollen, the muscles tired from contracting.

Her resistance was weakening. He pushed deeper into her throat. Through the thrumming in her ears, she could hear him groan.

Paine pulled out of her mouth, giving her a chance to catch her breath.

Leaning down, he wiped the tears from her cheeks and the spittle from her chin. Brushing the hair from her eyes, he said, "Goddamn, baby, you've never looked more beautiful. I've fantasized about having you kneeling before me, your mouth open and awaiting." His breath came in ragged, harsh gasps.

Mirage felt a sick pleasure at the raw lust and truth she heard in his words.

"You've taken half my cock. It's time to take the whole length down that pretty throat of yours."

Mirage started to shake her head vigorously, unable to speak. Her mind buzzed with conflicting emotions. She loved how powerless and dominated she felt as he forced his cock on her. The harder he bent her to his will, the fiercer, wilder, her response. It was an adrenaline rush, and like all good criminals, she was an adrenaline junkie.

Her mind screamed that it was wrong to feel this way. She tried to fight against her body's rising reaction.

"I love how your dark eyes glisten with tears each time the head of my cock hits the back of your throat," he growled as he gave the belt around her neck a slight tug.

An unwanted thrill shot through her body at his heated words.

Paine forced his cock once more into her mouth. The back of her head bumped against the wall.

The vibrations of her sobs and choking made him growl and thrust harder. He pushed the top of her head down and forward with his left hand as he held the soft length of the belt around her neck with his right.

Paine prodded the tip against the back of her throat. Using more pressure, he broke through her body's natural reflexes and forced his way deeper into the tight clenching heat of her mouth and throat.

Her throat felt like it was on fire. She couldn't breathe. Twisting and wrenching her arms, she tried to push at his strong thighs, to somehow dislodge him, instinctively wanting to fight him off.

"Stop!" he thundered.

Mirage immediately stilled, her fear of him overriding her need for breath.

After a few powerful thrusts, he pulled out, allowing her a gasping breath before plunging in deep again, crushing her nose against his abdomen.

"That's it, kitten, swallow my cock whole, take it all," he ground out.

Changing the position of his hands, he held onto the sides of her head. "I'm going to come down your throat," he warned before forcing her head up and down on his cock with increasing speed.

Mirage was powerless as he ruthlessly used her mouth for his own needs.

Paine grabbed the base of his cock as he stilled with it lodged down her tortured throat. Throwing his head back, the muscles in his neck bulged as he let out a satisfied roar of completion.

Mirage fell back on her heels. The taste of him in her mouth.

"Your turn now."

Paine grabbed her under her arms and lifted her up. Placing her body on the bed, he lifted her arms up and removed her T-shirt. The leather belt fell back down, lying heavy between her breasts. He gently pushed her shoulders till she fell back among the covers. He then swiped off her yoga pants. As usual, she wasn't wearing any panties. Kicking off his jeans, he joined her on the bed. Lying on his back, he lifted her pliable body till her knees straddled his face.

"Oh, I... I've never—"

"Shhh... I want to taste you. I want to feel your thighs clench against my head as you come."

Each time he spoke, the soft vibrations of his deep voice sent tremors through her cunt.

He parted her slick folds with the tip of his tongue and teased her clit.

"Oh, God!" she cried out as her fingers speared into his soft hair, pulling the wavy strands, crushing his head between her legs.

He continued to tease her with his tongue. Swirling

and tasting, he used his hands to pinch and pull at her erect nipples before running them down her back to grasp her ass and push her harder against his mouth.

Mirage's head fell back as her thighs pressed in. She could feel the pressure build. At that precise moment, Paine pulled on the belt still wrapped around her neck. The thick leather squeezed tight. She strained to breathe. Her fingers clawed at the strap, but he just pulled tighter. Her eyes fluttered shut as her cheeks suffused with color before going pale. She felt weightless. Her head swam. She was floating. Her whole body jerked as she came. Wave after wave of color and sound rushed over her as the last vestiges of air left her lungs.

Then everything went black.

CHAPTER 7

Istanbul, Turkey...two years earlier

THE SUMMER NIGHT air was stagnant and hot, the sun's setting offering little relief. There had been an atmosphere of suspended animation in the city all day. Mirage had just broken into the house of a high-ranking member of the Turkish Parliament who happened to be away on holiday. The Syndicate had instructed her to copy his hard drive and take photographs of anything she found in the hidden wall safe but not to steal its contents. They wanted no trace she had been there. She had already finished with the safe and was pulling the flash drive free from the computer when she heard the first round of gunfire.

Ducking low, she made her way out of the study and down the hallway to one of the front bedrooms. Leaning against the wall, she turned her head and hazarded a peek out the window which overlooked the main street below. The once-quiet night had erupted into chaos. Throngs of people were pouring into the street, shouting and waving Turkish flags.

Fuck me!

The Syndicate had sworn to her any possible coup wouldn't take place for at least another week. Mirage knew it was pointless to check her burner phone for information on any social media sites, the fastest option since it would take traditional media outlets at least a few hours to catch on. The Turkish government as well as the militants would both be disseminating their version of what was happening, neither completely true. She could be sure her main route out of the country, the Istanbul airport, was probably already or about to be shut down. These assholes always went straight for the airports.

Fuck me!

Just then she got a secure message from The Syndicate. They were sending one of their cleaners in. A man named Paine Darwin. Mirage was familiar with his work. He was a master thief like her but also branched out into the more violent jobs for The Syndicate. She must be in some serious danger if they were sending him to help. Still, she worked alone. She wasn't about to wait around for some guy she didn't know and, furthermore, didn't trust for shit, to come to her rescue.

Mirage set to work searching the rest of the house for a weapon and a plan.

* * *

THE GUNFIRE WAS GETTING CLOSER. The politician's residence was near the Bosphorus Bridge which seemed to be a central focal point for the angry crowds judging by her view from the rooftop earlier. She should barricade the front door, thought Mirage. This house might become a target for the bitter mob. Just as she was pushing a heavy chair across the marble foyer, the front door burst open. A furious man dressed in camouflage started screaming at her in Turkish and gesturing wildly. Mirage raised her hands to prove she was no threat as she stepped before him. Before she could utter a word in her defense, a spray of blood hit her cheek as the man's expression went blank. She leapt out of the way just as the dead man fell forward. Looking into the street behind, she saw a citizen with an M16. He raised his fist, yelled something in Turkish and ran down the street. Not knowing what else to do, she dragged the dead body inside away from the door and once more closed it, pushing the heavy chair on its side and in front as a barricade.

Then the bombing started.

Mirage dove under a round foyer entrance table. Curling her knees up to her chest, she covered her ears as clouds of dust and debris fell from the ceiling and the walls shook.

* * *

THE SHATTERING IMPACT of the bombs was emphasized by the sudden pounding on the front door. Mirage picked up the only weapon she could find, a steak knife from the kitchen. Crouching low, she waited to see if they would break through the barricade. It was better she stood her ground and observed whoever it was, since hiding in the house would put her at a disadvantage. She wouldn't have eyes on the situation. There was plenty of time to scatter once the door opened.

The door rattled from the impact. Once. Twice.

On the third strike, the chair shifted with a groan and the heavy wooden door was thrown open.

The streetlights from outside framed his large form as he took a cautious step forward. Surveying the room.

"Panama," called out the man.

Mirage relaxed slightly. That was the code word The Syndicate said Paine would use so she would know it was him. Still, she stayed in her hiding place. Watching.

He closed the door behind him and replaced the chair. She could see the moment he saw the corpse on the floor.

Then his eyes connected with hers.

He had the most mesmerizing gaze. Cold and intense. His eyes were so crystal blue they shone almost like silver. A strong, angular jaw, deep set eyes and dark, wavy unkempt hair gave him an appearance of casual authority, as if he was used to walking into a room and taking command. She marveled at how such a large and imposing man could be a thief. High-end thefts of jewels, information, even artwork, took agility. The ability to crawl through tight spaces, disappear into the sliver of a shadow, blend into the surroundings. She couldn't imagine this man blending in anywhere. His height alone set him head and shoulders above the average man.

She watched fascinated as he moved toward her with a silent, masculine grace.

"It wasn't me."

She didn't know why but she wanted him to know she hadn't killed that man. Although it probably would have served her purpose to make him think she had. Criminals had reputations to protect and uphold after all, and a little embellishment never hurt anyone.

"I wouldn't give a damn if it was, Mira."

Shocked, Mira stared at him. He called her Mira, not Mirage. Mira was dangerously close to her real name. A closely guarded secret she was certain even The Syndicate did not know. She searched his eyes for some form of recognition, perhaps from her past, but saw none.

"That's not my name," she said finally. "Everyone calls me Mirage."

"I'm not everyone. And I'm here to help you. The Syndicate sent me. So you can put down that steak knife you're clutching."

She watched as his face broke out into an arrogant smile. There were slight laugh lines around the tanned skin of his eyes. She marveled at that. She would have thought someone with his reputation would be more fierce and humorless, but he had laugh lines.

Disturbed by his immediate effect on her, she squared her shoulders as she placed the steak knife within view. "Who says I need help?"

Paine laughed. It was a deep, almost affectionate laugh. The hint of intimacy in that laugh rattled her.

Pushing him aside, Mirage crawled out from beneath the table. Standing before him, she straightened her spine to make her small frame seem as tall and imposing as possible.

Again the man laughed as he seemed to give her an appreciative look.

Brushing the dust off her palms and pants, Mirage once against straightened, hands on hips. "So what's the big plan to get us out of here?"

"We need to sit tight until tomorrow. I have a few contacts who say this will all blow over by then."

"So you just want us to wait around doing nothing?' she countered with an indignant tilt of her right eyebrow.

He gave her another one of his arrogant smiles and a seductive wink. "Well, I hadn't planned on doing nothing."

"In your dreams, pal," she smirked as she turned her back on him. "The bar is in the library. Might as well get drunk."

* * *

"Absolutely not!" she stated emphatically as a crystal glass of whiskey dangled loosely from her grip.

"Yes."

"No!"

"No is not an option, kitten."

She ignored his use of the endearment and the tiny flip in her stomach when he said it.

Placing her glass on the side table, she stood up, looking as regal as possible in her dusty clothes. "Fine. I choose dare."

"I don't know why we even decided to play this game. It's not like either of us will choose truth," he smirked. Motioning with his hand, he said, "Okay, you know the dare. Get to it."

Mirage thought for a moment. The dare was to demonstrate an outlandish, challenging move she'd had to use on any previous heist. Remembering that time in LA at the house with the crazy laser security system, she nimbly stood on her hands. Placing her legs straight in the air, she balanced her body for a moment before taking two steps forward on her hands and then slowly opening her legs into a full split.

She heard the scrape of his chair. Just as she was about to right herself, she felt his strong hands on her hips. He flipped her upright, her legs now wrapped around his waist. Her body flush with his. Running his hand up her back, he fisted it in her long curls. Using his grip on her hair, he forced her head forward to meet his brutal kiss.

His lips slanted over her own. She could taste the smoked wood essence of the whiskey on both of their tongues. He moved to kiss her jawline, then nip at her neck before sucking her earlobe into his mouth, gently biting down.

He whispered gruffly into her ear, "Jesus Christ, kitten. Promise me you will never do that move in front of any other man but me."

Still too taken aback by the violence of his kiss, she didn't respond.

He yanked on her hair. The sting sent an unexpected flash of desire through her body. Her shocked eyes clashed with his.

"I mean it. Promise me," he ground out, staring at her intently.

"I promise," she responded, and strangely enough, she meant it.

Without saying another word, Paine carried her out of the library and up the stairs. Turning into the first bedroom he found, he stripped the bed bare, laying her facedown upon it. He didn't even allow a moment's space between them before he'd covered her body with the heat and weight of his own.

The bombs had started again but neither cared. The world and all its chaos receded.

Sweat-sheened skin.

The scent of whiskey on their heated breaths.

The sting of his hand as he slapped her ass.

"Oh God! Fuck!"

Running his teeth along the whorl of her ear as he pressed his firm chest against her back. "Who owns you?"

A trill unfurled in her stomach. It was dirty, raw and possessive in a fucked-up way. His thick shaft stung as it tore into her tight body. A physical reminder that she was already owned, already possessed by him.

She submitted.

Licking her lips, she whispered. "You."

"Louder." His cock pressed in deep.

"You," she cried out. "You do."

"Say it. Beg me to fuck you," he ordered as he thrust harder.

Bracing her palms against the mattress, she pushed up, pressing her body into his, pressing his cock deeper. Reaching one arm up, she wrapped a hand around the back of his neck.

"Please, fuck me."

Cupping her breast, he pinched her nipple hard as his right hand slapped her ass.

"Oh, babygirl. You're mine now."

* * *

She'd pretended to be asleep when he left the next morning. He had left a note saying he was securing transportation out of the country and to be ready to go when he got back. She had already arranged her own way out.

She left before he returned.

She wasn't dumb enough to think she was anything to a man like Paine, despite his possessive nature the night before. Best to spare them both the awkward, morning-after conversation.

He would probably forget all about her...after all, this was a one-time thing. It was not like they would ever cross paths again.

CHAPTER 8

Present day

THE RUSTIC SMELL of wood burning and the feeling of being surrounded by soft warmth awoke Mirage from her dream.

She had been remembering her time in Istanbul, the moment she'd first met Paine, wondering if she could have known then how much he would later change her life, that he would tap into a part of her she hand't known existed. A dark and scary corner of her soul that liked to have her careful control taken away from her…by force. Mirage pushed those deep and troubling thoughts aside to take stock of her situation.

She knew better than to just suddenly open her eyes. Keeping her features calm, her breathing still, she brought all her senses into play. The smell of the fire and the heat on her cheeks reminded her they'd moved back into the living room. Soft wool caressed the bare skin of her legs and arms.

Correction, naked in the living room.

The feel of strong thighs under her own told her she must be on Paine's lap. There was a small, tingling flip in her chest at the thought. Mirage stopped breathing…to listen. Above the muted crackling of the fire, she could hear his soft, even breathing. Slowly, she opened her eyes to look at him through her thick, black lashes.

His features were smooth and even, lacking their usual angry animation. He was asleep.

Her dark eyes absorbed every detail. The slight scruff on his jaw. The lock of hair falling onto his forehead. The tiny tic in his left cheek as if he stirred in his dreams. She saw the thin silver chain around his neck. It hadn't been there earlier. He must have put it on after she'd passed out from…from the most intense sexual experience of her fucking life. Jesus Christ, the way he manhandled her. Forced her. Even now, she had to fight clenching her inner thighs in response.

Focus.

The blanket he had her wrapped in covered the lower portion of his chest so she couldn't see if there was the outline of the Raj Pink diamond. In addition to its thirty-million-dollar price tag, she had a strange, rather morbid, sentimental connection to the diamond. It was a talisman. A reminder to never let her emotions get the better of her. She wanted it back.

In one smooth motion, she pulled her right arm free of the blanket. Her left was pressed against the warmth of his body. With only the slightest whisper of a touch, she hooked the chain with her middle finger and gently pulled upwards.

"Like you, this diamond is mine now."

Paine's voice was thick and rough from sleep.

Her startled eyes connected with his amused ones as she dropped the chain.

"What makes you think I'm yours?"

One raven eyebrow quirked up over his left eye. "Do you want me to prove it again to you, babygirl?"

Mirage lowered her gaze, unable to match his intense, knowing one.

She played with a loose strand of yarn in the wool blanket. "Why?" she whispered.

Paine brushed a curl back behind her ear, caressing her cheek as he did it. "Why what, baby?"

"Why do you want me? Why are you doing this? Why haven't you kil—"

Paine pressed a finger to her lips.

"I have told you. You fascinate me."

Mirage's eyes widened in disbelief. "I fascinate you? I *fascinate* you? Do you have any idea how insane that sounds? I... I... ruined your reputation with that very pink diamond you wear around your neck. I... I... tried to kill you! We are in the middle of…. of… where the fuck are we?"

"Wales," offered Paine helpfully.

That threw Mirage off her rant for a moment. "Seriously? Wales?"

Paine shrugged. "Pearly's been to my London safe house for poker night."

She raised her hands in frustration. "Yes! Yes! See?

Exactly that. Pearly. I took out a contract to have you killed! And now we are hiding out in the middle of fucking Wales."

"What is your point, Mira?"

"Why on earth would I fascinate you? Why would you want me?"

"Sweetheart, if you don't know the answer to that, then any man who came before me should be shot."

Mirage bit her lip at the bitter reminder. Paine had shot Dev. Dev, the man she'd thought she loved. The man she'd risked it all to avenge. She would love nothing better than to throw Paine's words back in his face, but in her heart of hearts, she knew the truth. The truth which had always been there. Hiding in the dark, willfully ignored. Dev had never loved her. He'd just been using her, and worse, she had never truly loved him, just the idea of him.

It was a hard lesson to learn and one she was not going to forget.

Raising her chin, she said, "Listen. If all this is just some charade because you want something from me, some job you need done, I would rather you just come out and tell me what it is rather than pretend that we're in some kind of fucked up relationship."

Paine stood up with Mirage in his arms and tossed her lengthwise back down onto the sofa. The blanket about her dislodged. She could feel the scrape of his jeans against her soft skin as he straddled her hips. Placing his hands on the armrest, he loomed over her. His crystal blue eyes lit with anger.

"I want you to listen now and listen closely. There is nothing I want from you but this beautiful body and that even more beautifully fucked up, amazingly intelligent mind of yours. This is not some kind of pretend anything, baby. This is the real deal. You think you're the first person who has tried to kill me? Logan, the closet thing I have to a friend, has tried twice. So I've got news for you…it's not a deal breaker for me. Hell, that just makes me want you more. Let's just say I like your kind of crazy."

"I won't love you. I'm warning you now. I am absolutely determined never to fall for that trick again."

Paine threw his head back with laughter before lowering his lips to hers. Giving her a hard kiss, he said, "That's it. Just keep throwing those challenges at me."

"If you aren't the most exasperating, hard-headed—"

Her rant was cut short when she saw three crimson beads of light start to dance across his chest. Gun sights.

"Paine!" she screamed.

Throwing her body forward, Mirage knocked him off balance. They both tumbled to the floor just as the wood mantel over the fireplace exploded in a shower of splinters. Paine grabbed the blanket and threw it over her form to protect her from the wood shards. Covering her body with his own, he reached out with his right arm to flip the sofa on its side, dragging her behind its protective bulk. The crimson laser sights danced around the room searching for their target. Another bullet took out the only lamp in the small cottage's living room.

Mirage stayed low to the ground. "It's Pearly. He found us," she gasped, her breath short from shock.

Paine's brow wrinkled as he stared at the laser dots. He shook his head. "I don't think so. Pearly works alone. There are at least three shooters."

There was another volley of shots. A vase on the bookshelf at the end of the room shattered.

"He's also a hell of a better shot and doesn't waste unnecessary ammo," drawled Paine.

Mirage helped him turn the heavy, mahogany coffee table over and place it in front of the overturned sofa. They crouched behind its smaller surface.

"Maybe he brought help because it's you?" offered Mirage right before she covered her ears as another round of bullets lodged in the wall and broke the glass on a simple daisy print by the front door.

His mouth quirked up in a smile. "Why, Mirage, the threat of death does wonders for your disposition. I do believe that is the first time you have complimented me."

"Will you please be serious? Someone is shooting at us!" threw Mirage over her shoulder as she crawled on her hands and knees to peek around the sofa's edge.

Paine gave her a slap on her bare ass. "I knew you'd start to soften towards me."

"If you don't knock it off and come up with a plan, I'm going to throw you in front of one of those bullets," stormed Mirage even as her cheeks pinked from his teasing remarks and the feel of his hand on her ass.

"The plan is for you to crawl over to that door there. It leads down into the root cellar where it will be safer. I'll take care of the rest."

Paine crouched low and made his way to the kitchen. Mirage fumed. *I guess he assumes I'm going to obey without question*, she thought as she followed after him on her hands and knees, staying low and awkwardly clutching at the blanket over her shoulders.

As she rounded the corner, Paine was fishing something out of a kitchen drawer. She figured he would go for the knives, the only possible weapon. Which made it all the more confusing when he drew out a corkscrew. It was the kind with a small wooden handle running perpendicular to a vicious looking silver screw.

"What are you going to do with that?"

"Goddammit, Mira. I thought I told you to go down into the root cellar," he barked.

"Yes, and I'm marvelous at taking orders. What are you going to do with that?" Mirage asked again, unfazed by his anger as she nodded toward the corkscrew.

"Take care of business." His voice a dark monotone.

"Don't you want a knife?"

"No. Now do as I say. I don't want to be worried about you while I go out there."

"You're not going to kill them, are you?"

After a long pause, there was another spray of bullets. This time more sporadic. It was as if the shooters were getting impatient and had decided to just pepper the whole house with bullets and hope the occupants inside died of lead poisoning.

His blue eyes seemed to darken and harden. "They shot at you. Put *my woman* in danger. Yes, I'm going to kill them."

Mirage was startled by the fierce possessiveness of his words. He almost had her believing he actually cared for her. More unsettled by that thought than by the bullets whizzing over her head, Mirage turned to locate the door to the root cellar just as he was unlatching a window on the side of the house. She watched as he slipped one leg over the sill, hugging the wall then rolling out over the other side, slipping away into the darkness.

"Be careful, Paine," she whispered to the dark shadows beyond.

Unable to bear being down in the cold, dank root cellar where she wouldn't know what was happening, Mirage dragged the coffee table in front of her as she huddled in a corner of the living room between the wall and a heavy sideboard. She thought about trying to make her way into the bedroom to retrieve her clothes but then thought better of it. As a point of grim humor, she wondered what would be worse, being found dead naked or being found dead in that stupid cat T-shirt. Definitely the cat T-shirt.

For what seemed an eternity, she watched the macabre dance of three lights tracking over the walls and furniture. There were long pauses and then there'd be a hail of bullets, while other times just a single shot or two.

Then one light disappeared.

In horror, Mirage looked down at her front, expecting to see a crimson bead of light shining on her. A mark of death.

There was nothing there.

Then a second red laser dot disappeared.

Paine was slowly taking the shooters out…one by one.

Trying to still her ragged breathing, Mirage strained to listen, hoping for a hint of what was taking place outside in the darkness.

There was the sound of shouting. Then a few shots but none hit the house. It sounded as if the shooter was aiming at something outside. Paine.

Mirage's chest clutched at the thought of Paine lying dead in the mud outside. What a dizzying turn of events. Not two weeks ago, she'd wanted nothing more than that man cold in his grave. Now the very thought of it struck her with icy dread.

Silence.

Nothing but silence.

Mirage waited and waited.

Her head tilted to the right when she heard the soft scrape of a boot outside. Then a metallic click as the front doorknob turned. Belatedly, she realized she should have grabbed a knife to use as a weapon of her own. Too late now.

The door opened.

Mirage pushed against the wall. Willing herself invisible.

There was a cautious step inside.

The creak of an interior door opening, probably to the root cellar. The click of a light switch. A long pause.

Mirage held her breath.

The footsteps moved into the living room.

She ducked her head, trying to curl her body in, to hide behind the overturned coffee table.

"Here, kitty, kitty."

Mirage came flying out of her hiding place and ran straight into his arms. Uncaring as the blanket dropped to her feet, the warmth of his flannel enveloped her as his strong arms closed around her body. She buried her head in his shoulder, the scent of his cologne and the feel of his arms calming her. One of his hands slipped into her hair as he pulled her closer.

"Paine. I thought you were dead," she mumbled against his shirt.

Paine pulled her head away from his shoulder and looked into her eyes. He gave her a reassuring wink. "You're not getting rid of me that easily, baby." He then gave her a kiss on the forehead. Leaning down, he tossed a small black duffel bag to her. "Put these on. We have to get out of here."

Hurriedly taking the bag, Mirage looked inside. It was a change of clothing. And a gun.

She picked up the .38. "You had a gun?"

Paine just nodded.

"Then why the hell did you use a corkscrew?"

Paine shrugged his shoulders. "It seemed more sporting that way. Give 'em a fighting chance."

Mirage just shook her head at his arrogance as she gratefully slipped into the yoga pants and top, both in her signature black.

She watched as Paine surveyed the damage to the cottage. There wasn't a single wall that didn't have bullet holes in it. The asshats also seemed to have shot every delicate piece of glass or porcelain in the entire place.

"Pearly's going to be pissed."

"Because someone jumped on his contract?" asked Mirage.

"Nope, this is his house," Paine laughed, throwing an arm over Mirage's shoulders as they walked out of the cottage to their car hidden off to the side in some brush. Leave it to Paine to do something as arrogant and outlandish as breaking into the house of the person who was hunting him down, thought Mirage.

*　*　*

She watched as his phone cast an eerie glow inside his car. The contact he chose said only 'Logan.'

The phone started to ring.

Mirage looked at him quizzically. "Is that *the* Logan?"

Paine nodded as he steered the car around a dark curve with one hand, holding the phone in the other.

That was the Logan he meant? His closest friend who had tried to kill him twice?

"Hello, my friend. Still after your little black widow?"

"My little black widow is here with me now. You're on speaker. What have you learned?"

"Mirage? Hello, beautiful. Pleasure to make the acquaintance of anyone who tries to kill Paine," quipped Logan good-naturedly.

"It's nice to meet you as well," responded Mirage awkwardly.

"I always wondered. Was that you who made off with that lovely little 200 carat sapphire and diamond necklace from that private bank in Germany?"

"I…uh…well…" Mirage cast a glance at Paine. "A lady never tells, Logan."

Logan laughed. "I knew it was you. We should plan a heist together sometime. I'm sure it would be a successful partnership."

Mirage watched as Paine frowned. Taking Logan off speakerphone, he growled, "The only person she will be *partnering* with is me, you got that?"

Mirage could still hear Logan's chuckle. "You want to keep the little gem all to yourself. I understand."

"What have you learned?"

"Pearly dropped the contract. He's currently in South Africa. Said he couldn't kill you because you still owe him twenty bucks from our last poker game."

Paine smirked. "He might change his mind when he finds out what happened to his house."

Paine related to Logan the events at the cottage.

"Well, that brings me to my next point. You have yourself in some hot water, my friend. Remember my warning about The Syndicate?"

Paine had already suspected who was behind the hit crew. He should have known The Syndicate would find out about his and Mirage's…disagreement. They had eyes and ears everywhere. It was of no surprise to him that they would try to eradicate both him and Mirage despite their usefulness to them, before it became a problem dropped at their doorstep.

Paine nodded. "I thought as much. Not a crack group, though."

"They're scrambling. Not many want to take someone of your reputation on. Figure it's a suicide mission. So they are sending newbies into the field who don't know any better."

"That won't last. With my past, they'll eventually find someone willing to take the risk."

"Stay safe. I will let you know if I find out anything else."

Mirage didn't need Paine to tell her. She had overheard.

The Syndicate now had a contract out to kill both of them.

CHAPTER 9

Mirage grew thoughtful as they drove off into the night. "I'm sorry I got us into this mess."

Paine brushed off her apology. "I'm not."

"Really?"

"I met you during a chaotic disaster; it makes sense I would find you again in the middle of a chaotic disaster."

"Hey, it hasn't been proven yet that I caused that coup in Turkey," teased Mirage.

Their laughter broke the tension in the car. Only a pair of criminals would find humor while dealing with their current situation.

"Do you ever regret it?"

"Being a criminal?"

Mirage nodded.

"Nope. First person I ever hit was the man who had been beating on my mom for years. The moment I was big enough, I beat on him."

"Your father?"

Paine's fingers visibly tightened around the steering wheel. "I don't like to call him that, but yeah. Whoever said violence doesn't solve anything was lying. That piece of shit crawled away and never returned. That's when I became a thief. Needed to steal to help out my mother and younger brother. I started with cigarettes. I would steal cartons at a time and then sell the individual packs. My stealing gave them both a comfortable and stable life, so, no, I don't regret it for one moment."

Mirage smiled. "Me neither. As I see it, all we're really doing is transferring wealth. Stealing from one filthy rich person to give to another."

"Exactly," agreed Paine.

"Besides, I do my part. The money I get? I launder it through a charity that looks the other way. They take twenty percent."

Paine reached over and stroked her thigh. "I knew my little ice queen had a heart in there somewhere."

Mirage blushed at his teasing remarks. He really was the most intriguing man. A strange mix of anger and teasing humor. Of violence and tenderness.

"My name is… Miranda… Miranda Foster," she whispered. It felt strange to say her real name out loud. Mirage hadn't uttered her name or been called by it in over fifteen years.

Paine reached over and pushed a curl behind her ear before stroking her cheek. "My Mira."

"It's why I freaked when you called me that…it was like you knew who I really was," she offered, still looking down at her hands, too nervous and unsure to meet his gaze.

"I always knew who you were Mira. I just didn't realize I had the right name."

Mirage looked into his blue eyes, captivated. The spell was only broken when he had to turn his attention back to the road.

"Well, Miranda Foster, I'm Paine Darwin and it is a real pleasure to meet you."

Mirage felt a stab of disappointment. Summoning up a half-hearted smile, she said, "You don't have to tell me your real name if you don't want to. I don't expect it."

"That is my real name. Paine Darwin."

"Your mother named you Pain? P-a-i-n?"

"The way my mother tells it, it was a very long and painful labor, so it was the first word that popped into her head when the nurse asked my name. And it's Paine with an 'e,'" he corrected.

"Huh. I always just figured it was 'no e' Pain."

"That works too."

* * *

Two hours later, they pulled into a small, one-story hotel in some no-name town. It was surrounded by trees on two sides and a steep cliff dropping off on the other.

"We'll stop here for the night and strategize."

"Sounds good," said Mirage.

They checked in under the assumed names of Mr. & Mrs. Smythe. Mirage tried to ask for a separate room but that only got her a hard look from Paine.

After unlocking the door, he stood back and let her

pass over the threshold. It was a small, clean room. One bed.

Mirage hugged her arms around her middle. "I think I'm going to take a nice long hot shower."

"Want some company?"

"Not this time."

Mirage walked into the bathroom and locked the door behind her. Lowering the toilet seat, she sat down and rubbed her hands over her face. This was her mess. She'd brought this on them both with her petty revenge schemes and misplaced loyalty. Trying to contact The Syndicate and explain would only give away their location. No, she had to go right to the source. Where The Syndicate was based was a closely guarded secret. A secret she'd learned a few years ago from an operative they'd sent to collect some uncut emeralds she had stolen from the safety deposit box of some Mafia boss in Italy. The operative had been a little too excited to be in Italy and had sampled a little too much of the strong local wine. If she could break into their headquarters, perhaps she could learn something that she could leverage against them in return for her and Paine's lives? She would turn the tables on The Syndicate. Use the very skills they hired her for against them.

There was just one problem. Paine. He probably wouldn't go for the plan. Too dangerous. Besides, Mirage liked to work alone. She'd caused this mess. She should clean it up.

Despite her dramatic protestations earlier, Mirage knew she had lied to him...again. Deceiving him and herself about her feelings for him. Somehow, she had already fallen half in love with the man. Perhaps she had been half in love with him since their instant attraction that night in Istanbul. Normal one-night stands did not leave that much of a lasting impression; in fact, they were usually something a girl tried to forget and quickly.

Try as she might, she could not shake the memory of Paine. The man was arrogant, bossy and way too intense. He liked to be in control, something she couldn't stand giving up. They were completely wrong for one another and that was before her efforts to kill him were factored in. Everything about them shouldn't work or make sense and yet...she loved how he teased her. Loved the protective feel of his arms around her. Loved how he didn't take her crap and gave as good as he got.

And the sex...holy shit...the sex. It was so many levels of wrong which made it right for them both. Normal, vanilla missionary sex could never cut it for people who lived life on the edge like they did. Sex with Paine had all the elements of a great heist. Anticipation, danger, tension, euphoria. She secretly loved how he bent her to his will, made her beg for the pleasure and pain. The only way she ever would or could be completely submissive was to a strong, dominating man like Paine who took that submission from her by force. She needed to focus on all the reasons why she hated him. On how much he angered her. And not on the reasons why she was falling in love with him.

Oh, yes, she was already half in love with the man, which was why she had to get out now. Go back to her plan to disappear. She would clear Paine's name with The Syndicate and then vanish. It was the only way to protect herself. The way she felt about Paine didn't even come close to how she'd thought she had felt about Dev. It was like comparing an innocent schoolgirl crush to a full-blown passionate affair. And that scared the crap out of her.

Best to leave now before she fell any further. She was better off alone. Things were less complicated that way. Less intense. More in control.

That's the way she liked things, in control. Right? *That evil voice in her head whispered, you're lying again.*

Shaking off her wandering dark thoughts, Mirage stood up and turned on the shower.

Checking to make sure the door was locked, Mirage stepped up onto the toilet seat and quietly raised the frosted bathroom window. Swinging one leg over the sill, she stretched out her toes till her foot touched the ground. Mirage grimaced as it sunk a bit into the muddy, soft terrain. They had driven through a storm most of the night. She did not relish escaping through the wet and marshy woods, but she had no choice. She would keep under the cover of the trees until she reached a town or farmhouse where she could 'borrow' a car.

Swinging her second leg over, she dropped down to the ground.

"Going somewhere?"

Damn him!

Mirage put her hands on her hips. "I'm really hurt that you didn't trust me enough to assume I was taking a shower."

"You weren't and don't try to brazen your way out of

this one. We have a fucking hit out on us, and you're trying this bullshit disappearing act on me again."

His whole body practically radiated tension and anger, from his lowered brow to his crossed arms to his planted-foot stance. He was genuinely pissed.

Mirage did the only reasonable thing she could do...she ran.

Giving in to her pure panic response, Mirage feinted right then ran left. Veering around Paine, her nimble form took off for the tree line. Running through the haze caused by the cold drizzle, Mirage could hear his heavy footfall just behind her. Her leg muscles burned as she pushed them harder, struggling against the soft terrain as her feet slipped in the mud. Bursting through the tree line into the forest, she didn't dare look behind her lest she miss a low-hanging branch. Racing through the bramble of black branches and underbrush, she searched through the darkness for a place to hide. Her cheeks stung from the cold and from where small branches had whipped and scratched at her skin. Her breath came in short, ragged bursts as she strained to keep her small lead over Paine.

She never had a chance.

Mirage heard a deep, guttural roar. The warning cry of a feral beast. Her legs were knocked out from beneath her. Lowering her shoulder, she rolled into the fall. Paine's weight descended on her the moment her body hit the leaf-strewn ground. She lifted her knee between his spread legs. Reading her intent, he shifted his weight to the left. Mirage pushed with all her might. He fell to her side. As she tried to scramble away, he grabbed her arm and pulled her on top of him. The two rolled through the leaves as she clawed and thrashed against him.

Mirage started to weaken; she could not sustain her struggle against his superior strength. He pushed on top of her, straddling her hips. Capturing both her small wrists in his hand, he forced her arms above her head. Stretching out his weight, she could feel him pull at her pants till they were about her knees.

"Let me go!"

"Never."

* * *

HIS MIND WAS IN A RAGE. He actually wanted to hurt her with his cock, to pound into her so hard and fast she screamed in pain, begging him to stop. In some fucked up way, it was the only way he knew how to break through her icy exterior. Her relentless need to push him away.

Grabbing her by the sides of her face, Paine planted a fierce open-mouthed kiss on her lips. Pulling back, he rasped, "If I have to fuck you senseless every time you try to run from me, then so be it, but goddammit, you will learn there is no point in defying me in this."

Ripping at his jeans, he freed his cock. He didn't check to see if she was wet. He already knew she would be. Positioning his cock at her entrance, he thrust into her tight pussy to the hilt.

Her mouth dropped open in shock and pain from his powerful assault. Paine pulled his hips back, groaning when her body gripped his cock as he pulled free before thrusting back inside. Her body jolted from the impact.

She gave a soft moan. Charging ahead, Paine drove his cock in deeper with each thrust. Her body opened a little further with each forced movement.

"Oh, God. It hurts," she cried out as her cunt contracted around his girth. He could feel her inner muscles tremble as they stretched to accommodate his pounding shaft.

"Paine, it's too much," she begged. She tried pulling on her arms, but he only tightened his grip on her wrists, keeping her prone and helpless beneath him.

"No," he gritted out between clenched teeth.

A fine mist of cold rain began to fall through the trees onto their bodies as he fucked her like an animal in the woods.

"You're mine, Miranda. Do you understand me? Mine."

Paine could read the shift in her expressive dark eyes, desire storming to life as he forced her to submit, as she reacted to hearing her real name on his lips.

Savagely smashing into her hips, Paine came with a roar. His whole body tensed above her own as he spilled his seed deep within her. Branding her. The thought made the act even more carnal as he heard the cries of her own release echo across the dark forest.

* * *

PAINE CARRIED her all the way back to the hotel, never saying a word. He still seethed with anger and sexual energy.

When they entered the room, she could hear the hiss

from the shower which was still running. The sound damning her.

Without pause, Paine kicked in the locked bathroom door and carried her inside. Raising her arms over her head, he pulled off her now wet and muddied T-shirt, stopping to run his thumb over a scratch on her cheek.

His voice was low and dark when he commanded, "Take off your pants."

Not giving a thought to disobeying him, Mirage kicked off her dirtied sneakers and pulled off her yoga pants. She was now naked before him. She watched in silence as he stripped off his own damp and filthy clothes. Opening the shower door, he ordered her to get in. The cheeks of her ass brushed against his already hard shaft as she squeezed past him to step into the steam-filled chamber.

The hot water stung as it hit her chilled skin. Mirage hissed a pained breath through her teeth.

Paine stepped into the shower stall, filling the space. Despite her trepidation, Mirage marveled at the display of hard muscle on his tall frame. Lowering her eyes, she observed his thick shaft as it jutted forward, ready to claim her body again despite their earlier exertions. A tremor ripped through her body at the thought.

Still, Paine did not speak, just pierced her with those ice-blue eyes. He placed his large hand in the center of her chest, his fingers skimming her breasts. Slowly, he ran his hand down her front, applying just enough pressure to force her to take a step back to lean against the slick tiles. Turning his hand, he cupped her pussy.

Mirage gasped at the contact.

As he ground his palm against her flesh, Mirage rose up on her toes to avoid the pleasurable agony. She was still sore from the fucking she'd received in the woods.

Gripping his wrist, she begged, "Please, Paine, I'm still sore."

"Is my kitty-cat's pussy sore? Maybe I should kiss it and make it better?"

Mirage was at a loss for words when the powerful man knelt before her. Placing his hands on her inner thighs, he forced her to open her legs wider. She watched as his dark head bent close to her stomach. The first flick of his tongue against her sensitive nub sent a shock through her limbs. Desperately, her arms stretched out, searching for purchase. She latched on to the handle of the soap dish and the towel bar to keep her knees from buckling as he continued to lick and lave at her cunt. Shifting his right hand, he moved it between her legs and began to caress her with his two middle fingers. Rhythmically moving them back and forth in time with the swirling of his tongue, each time increasing the pressure. With each pass of his fingers over her cunt, he inched further and further back, till the tips were teasing her back entrance.

Mirage moaned as the tip of his middle finger circled her tight rosebud. Watching through half-closed eyes, she saw the muscles of his back stretch and tense as the hot water streamed down his body.

Between the pressure of his tongue and the subtle threat of more pain as he pushed his finger into her ass up to the first knuckle, Mirage's body spasmed. Her thighs clenched against his head.

"Oh, God! Fuck!" she screamed as she came.

Paine rose to tower over her.

"Turn around. Hands on the wall."

"I-I can't Paine. I'm still sore from earlier," she complained, only half lucid, still in the throes of her orgasm.

Grabbing her shoulders, he forced her to obey his command. Mirage's breasts were pressed into the tiles as Paine's hands lowered to her hips, pulling them toward him so that her back arched.

Leaning in close, he whispered into her ear, "It's a good thing I'm not planning on fucking your pussy then."

"No!" cried out Mirage as she tried to turn back around.

Paine placed a large hand between her shoulder blades, keeping her in place. Mirage then felt a burst of stinging heat as he gave her ass three brutal swats.

"You don't have a choice. You know what the punishment is for disobeying me, kitten."

CHAPTER 10

After admiring the faint blush on her right ass cheek caused by his hand, Paine picked up one of the small bottles of conditioner the hotel provided.

"Reach back and open your ass cheeks for me," he ordered.

Mirage whimpered.

Paine placed a threatening hand on her still-heated right cheek. "Do you need another reminder to obey me?"

"No," she gasped as she tentatively reached back and tried to grasp her wet skin.

Paine grabbed her wrists and forced her arms back further. "Place your fingers in the seam and pull them apart."

Mirage did as she was told, opening her bottom for him.

Unscrewing the cap on the conditioner, Paine drizzled the contents down the seam of her ass and over her small, puckered hole. He watched the iridescent pearl liquid cover her pink skin as Mirage jumped up onto her toes from the contact of the cool liquid on her warm body.

Fisting his cock, heavy with arousal, Paine took a step forward.

"Were you a bad girl?"

Mirage nodded yes.

"Say it," he growled.

"I was a bad girl," she groaned as she turned her head to press her forehead against the tiles.

"And what happens to bad girls who run away?"

"Please don't," begged Mirage. "It will hurt too much."

Paine cupped her right ass cheek and squeezed hard.

Mirage screamed and rose up on her toes again.

"I asked you what happens to bad girls who run away."

"They get punished."

"How do they get punished, Mira. I want to hear you say it."

"They get a cock in their ass."

"That's right, baby. They get the full ten inches."

Mirage whimpered.

Planting his feet wide, Paine grasped his cock and positioned it between her ass cheeks. Pressed the tip against her entrance. Her body clenched tightly closed. He pushed harder.

"Let me in, baby. Let me into that tight ass of yours."

"I can't," she whispered.

"You will," he ground out.

Shifting his hips forward, he ruthlessly pressed the bulbous head of his cock inward, watching as the conditioner-slicked opening began to weaken from his assault.

After a moment, the head popped in despite her resistance.

Mirage cried out, her hands clawing at the tiles as her thigh muscles tightened.

Paine gritted his teeth against the wave of sick pleasure that washed over him the moment her body submitted to him. He thrust forward, burying half his cock in her heat.

"Ow! Ow! Please take it out! Take it out!" begged Mirage.

Paine was deaf to her pleas. Pulling his hips back slightly, he pounded into her a second time, forcing her to take all ten inches at once.

Mirage screamed.

He continued to thrust, the tight clench of her ass around his cock spurring him on.

"Arch your back," he commanded with a slap to her ass for emphasis.

Mirage immediately complied. Arching her back, she pushed her hips further onto his cock. They both moaned in unison.

Paine wrapped his arms around her and cupped both her breasts. Squeezing the soft flesh, he pinched each pert nipple with his fingers.

Plunging his shaft deep inside her body, he rasped against her neck, "Tell me. Tell me how it feels."

"It hurts. It feels full. There's so much pressure," she moaned.

"But you like it don't you? You like being taken against your will. Used. You like the pain of submitting."

"Fuck! Oh, God," she moaned as she instinctively pushed her hips back.

"Tell me, baby. I want to hear you say it."

"Yes! Fuck! Yes! Fuck me, Paine. Make it hurt."

Driving into her hard and fast, Paine kept his left hand on her breast while he moved his right to her throat. Gently squeezing, he tilted her head back to rest on his shoulder as he leaned into her. Her body started to rock and tremble in his strong grasp. She was close. He could feel it.

Moving his left hand, he caressed her cunt before forcing two fingers into her sore and swollen passage.

Mirage bucked in his arms. Her hands reached out to hold onto his wrists as he rocked into her ass. Paine lifted his torso, standing upright. With her petite frame still clenched in his grasp, he lifted her bodily off the tiled floor. The weight of her body came down on his cock as he stood with her back flush against his front.

"Oh fuck!" she screamed as she came.

Paine thrust once more before releasing inside her.

They both collapsed against the tiled wall. Their heavy breathing and the hissing rush of water from the shower the only sounds.

Turning in his arms, Mirage cuddled up against his shoulder. Giving him a shy smile, she said, "I will have to misbehave more often."

Brushing the wet curls back from her cheek, he gave her a quick kiss on the lips. "Baby, if you misbehave any more than you already do...you may just succeed in killing me," he teased with a smile.

* * *

"That is not at all how it happened!" protested Mirage.

"That is exactly how it happened," argued Paine.

They were sitting naked in bed eating Chinese takeout. Paine had also gotten them some wine which they sipped from the clear plastic cups provided by the hotel.

Grabbing a bite of lemon chicken from the container in her hand with his chopsticks, Paine said, "You just don't want to admit you were instantly seduced by my charms."

"Despite what you may think of your *charms*, I did not just fall into bed with you that night!" said Mirage as she reached over to grab some of his lo mein with her own chopsticks.

They were reminiscing about the infamous night they first met in Istanbul.

"You *tried* to get in my pants, but if I recall, I told you to go scratch. It wasn't until you got me drunk on whiskey that I gave in," said Mirage.

"As I recall it, you did that move where you spread your legs and begged me to fuck you."

"I was showing you a move from one of my heists!"

"A move that required you to stand on your hands and open your legs…wide?" asked Paine as he quirked a disbelieving eyebrow at her.

Mirage took a dainty sip of her wine as her cheeks blushed pink. "Well," she said, flustered, giving him a dramatic roll of her eyes.

"Just what I thought," smirked Paine. "Why did you leave the next morning? I left you a note saying I would return."

Mirage shrugged her shoulders as she played with the hem of the sheet. "I'm not very good with relationships and interacting with people. I'm alone a lot. I think the only reason why my relationship with Dev worked as long as it did was because he was actually rarely around and always just told me what I wanted to hear. It's hard to get spooked into running away by a man who sets such a low bar with no real expectations of you. Besides, I didn't think I was anything more than a convenient one-night stand to you and wanted to avoid an awkward conversation the next day."

Paine crooked his finger under her chin and forced her to look at him. "Well, you were wrong about that, and I plan to always be around from now on, so you better get used to it. And every time you run away...I will give chase, kitten. Every time."

Mirage blushed a richer hue of pink at his possessive words.

"And it was your loss. I brought back Yumurtali pides that morning," provoked Paine.

"I love pides!" exclaimed Mirage. Pides were a Turkish savory pastry with smoked meat, tomato, cheese and sometimes a baked egg.

"I figured you might. Do you have any idea how difficult it was to find pides while a fucking coup was still going on?"

"Sorry," offered Mirage sheepishly as she bit into an egg roll.

"Speaking of the coup, how the fuck did you manage to vanish out of the country like that? The airports were still closed and the military had the whole city on lockdown."

Mirage gave him a sly look. "There is a reason why they call me Mirage...because I got skills."

"I'll show you skills," growled Paine playfully as he tossed the egg roll she was eating over his shoulder and leaned in for a kiss.

*** * ***

Much later, they were no longer able to avoid the world outside. They had to discuss their current predicament with The Syndicate—the kill contract that loomed over each of their heads.

"I have an idea but I warn you, you're going to hate it," said Mirage.

"Maybe not. Everyone knows no one beats you when it comes to a good, well-thought-out plan," responded Paine with only the barest hint of a sarcastic reference to her well-laid plan of revenge against him.

Mirage told him of her idea to break into The Syndicate's headquarters and steal enough evidence against them to blackmail them into leaving her and Paine alone.

CHAPTER 11

"I hate it," declared Paine.

"I knew you would," sighed Mirage.

"You're goddamn right I would. I'm not letting you put yourself in that amount of danger. There has to be another way."

"There isn't."

"I can protect you, you know that," said Paine as he cupped her jaw, his eyes sincere.

"But for how long? The Syndicate won't stop until we're dead. This is the only way."

Paine dropped his hands and turned away.

"You know I'm right," said Mirage.

"That doesn't make this any easier," ground out Paine.

At that moment, she knew she had won him over. They would begin to plan the most dangerous heist of either of their careers...with the highest of stakes.

* * *

"Tight as a nun's ass," quipped Paine.

"I know."

"That's what John Gotti said when someone proposed robbing the vaults of the Diamond District...tight as a nun's ass."

"I know," repeated Mirage.

After returning to London to grab clothes, supplies, stashed fake I.D.s, and cash, Paine and Mirage *borrowed* a car and drove onto the Eurotunnel Le Shuttle train to cross the channel into France. From there, they made their way up the coast to Antwerp, Belgium. Flying would have been faster, but neither wanted to risk getting nabbed by Heathrow's facial recognition software, which they were certain The Syndicate had access to and was probably monitoring.

They had been alternating between planning the heist and arguing about the heist the entire way.

The Syndicate's headquarters were located in the Diamond District of Antwerp, in what was called the Diamond Square Mile. It was the most secure three blocks in the world. The three main streets, Schupstraat, Hoveniersstraat and Rijfstraat, were all closed to traffic and protected by armed guards and fourteen knee-high, ram-proof, steel cylinders which rose out of the ground to block any car trying to enter. Not that bringing a car into the narrow, antiquated streets would do much good in a heist, but it also meant whatever equipment they needed would have to be carried on their backs in inauspicious backpacks.

"They have a LIPS vault," stated Paine.

Mirage dismissed his comment with a wave of her hand. "At least it's not a Fichet!"

The Dutch safe manufacturer LIPS created some of the most secure vaults in the world. They were good, but not as good as the British manufacturer, Fichet. The fact that it was a LIPS made the heist difficult but not impossible.

From her wine-soaked, loose-lipped operative back in Italy a few years ago, Mirage had learned not only the location of The Syndicate's base of operation but also the name of their shadow company. After that, it was just a matter of a little computer hacking to learn where that company was insured. All companies located in the Diamond Center, a group of business offices and vaults in the center of the Diamond District, had massive amounts of wealth that required vaults and extensive security. This, in turn, required them to have insurance inspections and detailed security plans. Fortunately for Mirage, that detailed plan was in the shadow company's file with their insurer. They knew how many guards to expect, the type of vault and all about the motion and laser detectors, as well as the video cameras.

"The School of Turin took two years to plan their heist, and we're trying to plan ours in two weeks," said Paine.

The School of Turin was a group of thieves who had robbed the Diamond Center about a decade ago. It was the same building they would be targeting. The Syndicate was smart. They were hiding all their wealth and criminal activities in plain sight among some of the most heavily secured, legitimate companies in the world. It was brilliant really. In any other city, even New York, it might have raised eyebrows to see an armored BMW pull up with a trunk full of gold bars. But in Antwerp's Diamond District, that was just a Tuesday morning.

"The School of Turin needed to make off with a truckload of jewels and cash. We don't," reasoned Mirage.

Conversing and slowly building trust in one another over the last two weeks, they had learned they had both been smart with their criminal earnings. Paine had about fifteen million stashed away in various countries and Mirage had about twenty million, a fact she liked to repeatedly remind Paine of. "Does this mean I would be your sugar mama?" she would tease.

This wasn't about grabbing more wealth. It was about securing enough damning information to make The Syndicate back off.

"So you think once we have shit on them, The Syndicate will just walk away instead of doubling their efforts to kill us?" asked Paine.

Mirage shrugged her shoulders. "It would only take a few seconds to launch that information into the world via social media and they know we could make arrangements for that to be done the moment someone pulls a trigger. It would be safer to just keep us alive and monitor us."

"I agree. Hey, didn't you do a job in Antwerp not too long ago?"

Mirage peeked at him through her eyelashes, "Allegedly...but *if* I had, it was one of the smaller diamond businesses just outside the Diamond Square Mile."

* * *

"Repeat it back to me," ordered Paine.

"We've been over this. I got it."

Paine tucked a dark curl behind her ear before cupping her face in his hands. "I'm not taking any chances, baby. Now repeat it back to me."

"If we get caught, you are going to tell the police I'm an employee of one of the offices and your hostage. I'm then to contact Logan and let him know what happened so he can put a plan in place to get you out of prison."

"Good girl."

"But we're not going to get caught."

"Do you know how many times I have been sent into a country to retrieve an operative for The Syndicate who thought the same damn thing? No one expects to get caught, Mira." He placed a quick kiss on her lips. "Let's go."

Grabbing their backpacks, Paine and Mirage headed out into the dark, still night. They had rented an apartment just a few blocks away from their target. It came with the type of landlord who took cash and didn't ask a lot of questions, so they only had a ten-minute walk to the Diamond District. Paine had his arm around Mirage and they chatted animatedly so if they passed any police, they would look like a couple out on a date.

"You know, we haven't even been on a date and you are already talking about the future," observed Mirage.

"As soon as the blood-thirsty criminal masterminds who want us dead are brought to heel, I will take you out for dinner and a movie. How does that sound?" Paine took a playful bite at her ear.

Mirage felt a warm glow in her chest. She knew he

was probably teasing, but the thought of going out like a normal couple on a normal date appealed to her.

There were cameras and security kiosks monitoring all the entrances. Luckily for them, the C Block building where The Syndicate's vault was located had a garage door that was not in the security guard's line of sight. After a bit of reconnaissance earlier, they had captured a photo of the type of garage door opener that was used for it. After that, it had just been a matter of using an electronic scanner to figure out which one of the possible one thousand twenty-four radio frequencies the garage door opener used to make their own remote. Paine hit the garage remote button as they approached. Looking to the right and left of the silent street to make sure they weren't observed, they quickly slipped into the garage.

Paine knelt before the first locked door. Reaching into his backpack, he pulled out an L-shaped torque wrench and inserted it into the bottom of the keyhole. He then took a thin pick with small teeth and inserted it into the keyhole as well. Carefully dragging the pick back and forth, he waited for the pins of the lock to set.

"Are you setting up a picnic?" whispered Mirage.

"Patience."

Mirage crossed her arms. Finally, after a few more seconds, there was a barely perceptible metallic click. Paine turned the knob and motioned for Mirage to enter. She pointed to her watch. "Hmmm... nine seconds. I could have done it in six."

Paine gave her a playful swat on the ass.

"All right, your turn. And I'm timing you," said Paine as he prepared to set the stopwatch on his wrist.

Mirage knelt before the second door. This small, empty guards' room contained the key for the vault. A LIPS vault had a one-foot thick door of iron and steel protected by a four digit combo code, a magnetic lock and a key. The key was just over a foot long so it was too cumbersome to be kept anywhere but near the vault. Giving Paine a wink to start the clock, she quickly inserted her own torque wrench and pick.

Five seconds later the door sprang open.

"Show off," whispered Paine.

Mirage stuck her tongue out at him.

After a quick search, they found the key and made their way down the narrow hallway. Mirage reached into Paine's backpack for the can of silly string. As soon as they were within view of the vault, she handed the can to him. Pressing their backs against the wall, they crept to just below the first motion camera, attached to the ceiling. Using the silly string, Paine disabled the camera. He then took out the next two and the three video cameras. They took slow and careful steps toward the vault. Just because the motion detectors were covered didn't mean they wouldn't react to quick and large movements.

They both knelt before the vault's massive iron and steel door. After pushing the key in place, Paine pulled out a drill and some fiber optic cable while Mirage worked on the magnetic alarm. It was a simple contraption. There was one magnetic plate on the door and one on the jam. When they connected, they completed a circuit and a simple alarm was set. Mirage carefully placed a heavy metal bar over both magnetic plates. She made eye contact with Paine as a signal she was about to go. If all went well, the metal bar would pull the magnetic plates off the door and bypass the alarm. The trick was both plates had to stay connected and be dislodged from the door at the same time. If the plates disconnected even slightly, the alarm would trip.

Mirage held her breath. Paine gave her a reassuring nod. Counting to two, she pulled on the metal bar. The magnetic plates came off the door with a soft popping sound.

They both waited.

No alarm.

Mirage smiled.

Now it was Paine's turn. Handing a pair of plastic goggles to Mirage, he put his own on and started to drill. It was the loudest part of their whole operation, so it needed to be done as quickly as possible. Drilling through the keyhole would give them access to a narrow shaft through the one-foot iron and steel door. The key plate gave way. Paine threaded the fiber-optic cable through the keyhole and turned on the camera. Mirage's hand was at the ready over the combination pad. As soon as the camera was in place, Paine would be able to read the combination off the back of the locking mechanism on the inside of the vault door.

He read off the numbers. Mirage typed them in.

The sound of several heavy bolts sliding on greased rails greeted their efforts. Some turns of the large metal wheel, and the vault door slowly slid open.

The inside of the vault was protected with light sensors. They both put on their headlamps and turned them on. The usual white light was covered with a red lens. Red was the closest color on the visible light spectrum to infrared and could be used to trick the security system if you were careful with your movements.

Paine gave Mirage an assessing look as her features were bathed in crimson red light. "That reminds me. Where is that red lipstick I bought you?"

"I still have it. Why?"

Usually, she always wore red lipstick. It was her signature look and the only real makeup she used, but the last two weeks they'd been trying to blend in more, so bright red lips were out.

"I just thought about how I wanted to celebrate when this is over."

Mirage had a sudden vision of herself on her knees sucking Paine's cock as she left lipstick marks up the shaft. The thought made her bite her lip in anticipation.

"Will you focus please?" she remonstrated.

They found themselves in a large room. Each wall was covered with brushed metal safety-deposit boxes of varying sizes. In the center was a long, polished wood conference table with seats. Since boxes required both a key and a combination, it was easier to just break the deadbolt on each one.

With each of them taking a side, they began to systematically pop the boxes open.

"Remember, make sure to grab any silver flash drive with the letter M etched on it. That's more than likely one of my jobs, and I stole a lot from foreign governments for them," said Mirage.

"Got it," responded Paine.

They couldn't possibly know anything specific to look

for. They would just grab as much information as they could along with whatever looked incriminating enough. As they emptied the contents of each box onto the floor, the room became littered with priceless jewels, gold coins, uncut diamonds, salacious photographs and documents.

"Don't be afraid to grab anything sparkly that catches your eye," quipped Paine.

Mirage pulled another box free and dumped it onto the floor. Bending down to rifle through the contents, she looked up. "Hey, that reminds me. I want my Raj Pink diamond back!"

"You mean *my* Raj Pink diamond?" asked Paine with feigned innocence.

Mirage narrowed her eyes at him. "How about we compromise...our Raj Pink diamond?"

Paine gave her a seductive wink. "Deal."

Mirage was still having a hard time believing the strange turn of events. She now accepted that she was head over heels truly in love with Paine. Not the idea of Paine or some silly fantasy about what a relationship should be, but the real deal. Never in a million years had she thought she could so easily fall into step with someone. Her relationship with Dev hadn't even come close. Even this heist, she would have thought it was their hundredth and not their first, they worked so well together. To think that she would relish having a partner in crime. Literally. She still got scared. Every now and then, there would be this cold pit in her stomach. She would worry about having to return to those solitary days where her life was a controlled vacuum devoid of any real feeling or passion instead of the beautiful chaos which surrounded her and Paine, but then he would grab her by the hips and say something outrageously arrogant and possessive and warn her as he always did...that she was never getting rid of him.

"We should start to wrap this up, kitten. There's got to be something in all these flash drives we can use," said Paine as he held open his backpack. It was filled with at least a hundred flash drives, many of them silver. "Look at all those silver drives. You were a very busy, very naughty girl."

Mirage flashed him a smile as she caught the seductive turn of his thoughts. "Yes. I was a very bad girl."

Paine took a step toward her. Wrapping his arm around her, he pulled her close. Leaning in, his lips brushed hers. "Looks like I'm going to have to punish you."

Mirage's inner thighs clenched. Between the adrenaline rush of the heist, the threat of getting caught and Paine's masculine presence, her blood was already running high and hot.

"You'll have to catch me first!"

Mirage bolted out of the vault. The sudden movement set off the alarm.

Paine laughed as he gave chase.

It was part of their plan to set the alarm off. They wanted The Syndicate to know of the theft as soon as possible. The sooner they knew they were compromised, the sooner they would be willing to call off the hit and negotiate with Paine and Mirage.

* * *

They didn't even return to the small apartment. Hopping in a car they had staged a few blocks away just outside the Diamond District, they were already making their way through the labyrinth of old streets before they heard the first police siren. Hours later when they were far outside of the city on a dark country road, Paine pulled the car over.

"Why are we stopping?" asked Mirage as she turned to look out the back window for any sign of trouble before turning back to Paine.

He held up a tube of crimson red lipstick. "We did it, baby. Time to celebrate."

Giving him a seductive laugh, Mirage whipped off her T-shirt before leaning in to kiss him.

CHAPTER 12

Istanbul, Turkey - Three months later

WALKING from the cool interior of the villa into the bright sunshine, Mirage lowered her sunglasses over her eyes and scanned the pool area for Paine. The cedar wood patio felt warm beneath her feet as she made her way to the northern corner which was shaded by the dark green leaves of several hazelnut trees.

"Coffee." Mirage handed him a warm mug before settling onto the thick cushions of the lounge chair next to him.

"Thanks, love."

Turning her head to the side, she glimpsed at the open laptop on the small table between them.

"Still reviewing the Turkish coup files?"

"I still find it hard to believe The Syndicate was actually involved in that mess. Makes sense now why they sent you to basically gather any evidence of their involvement."

"Told you I didn't start the coup," joked Mirage.

Paine smiled, leaning over to push an errant, glossy blonde curl behind her ear as he always liked to do, before returning to the computer.

Mirage stretched and tilted her head back to catch the sun's warmth. Her thoughts wandered over the whirlwind events of the last three months. They'd been barely out of Antwerp before The Syndicate reached out to them. Mirage informed them that in the event of the death of either her or Paine, the flash drives would immediately be distributed to every major government head and corporation around the globe. The Syndicate would be completely exposed. Ruined.

The Syndicate immediately changed their tune, apologizing for the miscommunication regarding the kill contract. Stating it was the ill-advised, over-zealous efforts of a low-level employee. Whether they were a mastermind criminal organization or a big public corporation, companies were all the same. Pass the buck and deflect blame.

Once the threat of a bullet to the head was gone, Mirage went about fixing the damage she had wrought. Since they were already in Belgium, the first thing they did was break into the museum in Brussels and steal back the fake Vermeer. She then arranged to have the original stolen one, which she had tucked away in one of her flats in London, returned to Paine's client. After that, the rest was just a matter of a well-placed word here and a little money there and Paine's reputation was restored.

Curiously, Mirage was surprised at how much she enjoyed working with Paine. She'd always thought she had to work alone to stay in complete control. Through Paine she was learning to loosen the reins a bit, that life was more fun when you let in a little chaos. Oh, she still pushed his buttons. Still loved to make him angry. She was addicted to the adrenaline rush of pleasure and pain that came from making him chase her. The feel of his hands when he forced her down on the bed, ruthlessly pushing her legs open wide so he could drive into her. Oh yes, that part of their relationship would never change.

The harsh ring of Paine's cell interrupted her seductive train of thought.

"Hey, Logan."

"Hello, Logan," chimed in Mirage.

"Mirage says hello."

"Tell the black widow I say hello back," Logan returned.

"What's up?"

"Well, they've doubled their offer. They're willing to split the take fifty-fifty if you and Mirage agree to do the job together."

The Syndicate had been contacting them relentlessly over the last few months. There were few thieves who had Paine's special skill set or Mirage's abilities, and they were having a hard time filling the void left by their absence. As with most things, money forgave all ills. The Syndicate wanted them back in the field. In an amusingly ironic way, the fact that they had successfully broken into one of the most secure vaults in the world actually put them in higher esteem with The Syndicate, despite the fact that it was their vault Paine and Mirage had robbed.

Mirage sat up and started to nod her head. Their time at the pretty yellow stucco villa in the hills of Istanbul had been lovely, but she was anxious to get back to the excitement of planning their next heist.

Paine laughed. "Well, it looks like the answer is yes. We'll head back to London by the end of next week."

"Now that business is out of the way, I heard you popped the question to the black widow. Chloe wants to know if you got down on one knee like a gentleman?" asked an amused Logan.

"No. I told her she was mine, and I wanted to make it official," responded Paine gruffly, lowering his voice and trying to turn his shoulders away from Mirage so she wouldn't hear his response.

She heard.

Mirage hopped up. "That's not at all the way it happened!"

Snatching the phone from Paine's grasp, she said, "Logan? He's lying to you. He got down on one knee. There were tears in his eyes when he told me how much he loved me!"

Her speech came in excited gasps as she was running around the pool trying to avoid Paine's clutches. Mirage stuck her tongue out at him as she tossed the phone in the air and then jumped in the pool right as he was about to catch her.

Snatching the phone out of midair, Paine said an abrupt, "Gotta go. I have to teach a bad kitten a lesson."

He hung up the phone and tossed it aside before diving into the pool after her.

Mirage gave out a shout of frightened excitement as she tried to swim away.

Paine grabbed her around the waist, forcing her legs to straddle him as they floated in the clear blue water.

Mirage leaned back and tried to splash him. "Let me go, you villain!" she said with dramatic flourish.

"Never." His mouth descended, capturing her lips for his own.

How the proposal really happened...

MIRAGE AWOKE to a warm breeze floating over her bare skin. The breeze ruffled the white gauze curtains which led to the balcony overlooking the Arno River in Florence. She stretched her arms above her head, smiling when she saw the crimson silk tie still wrapped around her wrist from the night before. Shifting her hips, she grimaced slightly at the soreness between her legs. No doubt she had bruises on her hips too from where his strong hands had held her down while he thrust into her from behind. She loved the ruthless violence of his love-making. It was so unrestrained and passionate, so unlike the rigid control of her former, now-forgotten existence.

As she moved, she felt something shift between her breasts. Sitting up, she lifted the gorgeous, princess cut pink diamond which now dangled from a silver chain around her neck. As she did so, she noticed a matching large pink diamond on her ring finger.

"Do you like them, kitten?"

Mirage looked up to see Paine leaning against the balcony door. He was dressed in only a pair of blue silk pajama bottoms. His muscular chest with its swirls of hair were on full, enticing display. So were the crescent moon bite marks she had left on his shoulder.

"The Raj Pink diamond?"

Paine stepped into the room to sit on the edge of the bed. With the back of one knuckle, he traced the slope of her breast before picking up the diamond pendant. "There was no way I was going to sell it. I decided to have it cut into a ring and necklace for you."

Mirage held up her left hand, shifting it to and fro to catch the early morning sunlight, sending rainbows of crystal color dancing across the ring. She bit her lip. "Does this mean you…"

Paine placed a finger under her chin and forced her gaze to meet his. "You're mine, Miranda. If I have to chase you around the world proving that fact to you, then I will, but I would much prefer to prove it to you here in bed."

Paine pulled on her hips till she was lying flat, then placed the warm weight of his body over hers. Digging his fingers into her hair, he brushed his lips against her neck. "Who owns you?" he asked playfully as he shifted lower, scraping his teeth against her pert nipple.

Giving him a wicked grin, she said, "Bite me."

Closing his teeth painfully on her flesh, he gladly accommodated her.

Mirage arched her hips and groaned before placing a

hand along the rough stubble of his jaw, saying, "I'm yours, Paine."

"Do you love me?" he asked.

"I do," she responded without hesitation.

"Good. Remember those two little words because you will be saying them again soon," he teased as he nibbled and licked the smooth skin of her neck.

"I don't remember you actually asking me to marry you." Mirage's eyes sparkled with humor. She loved bantering with him.

Paine lifted up to straddle her hips. Grabbing her wrists, he stretched them above her head. Using the tie that was still around her left wrist, he secured them both to the headboard before running his hands over her breasts and down her stomach. Then placing his hands on either side of her head, he leaned down to rasp darkly against her lips, "I'm a thief. I never ask. I take what I want."

Mirage moaned as she tilted her hips upward. "Take me, Paine." Then, with a seductive twist to her lips, she whispered, "Make it hurt."

THE END.

ABOUT ZOE BLAKE

Zoe Blake is the USA Today Bestselling Author of the romantic suspense sagas The Diamanti Billionaire Dynasty & The Cavalieri Billionaire Legacy inspired by her own heritage as well as her obsession with jewelry, travel, and the salacious gossip of history's most infamous families.

She delights in writing Dark Romance books filled with overly possessive billionaires, taboo scenes, and unexpected twists. She usually spends her ill-gotten gains on martinis, travels, and red lipstick. Since she can barely boil water, she's lucky enough to be married to a sexy Chef.

ALSO BY ZOE BLAKE

THE SURRENDER SERIES

An Enemies to Lovers Romance

Ruthless Surrender

I know her darkest secret and am just ruthless enough to use it against her.

Whether she likes it or not, I'm the only one who can help her, but I do nothing for free.

My price is her complete surrender.

She can hate me all she wants, as long as she pays with her body.

And if she tries to run?

That will just cost her more.

Rebellious Surrender

First, she tried to kill me.

Then she ran.

Hunting her down will be my pleasure and her pain.

Nobody defies me and gets away with it, especially not her.

My pretty captive is about to learn her rebelliousness has consequences.

I'll settle for nothing less than her complete surrender.

Reckless Surrender

Her first mistake was lying to me.

Did she actually think I would let her get away with this deception?

I was going to make her pay for every lie that slipped from those gorgeous lips.

She may think this is just a game of teacher and naughty schoolgirl, but I have a surprise for her.

I only play games I can win, and my prize will be her complete surrender.

Relentless Surrender

She's mine… she just doesn't know it yet.

Stubborn and feisty as hell, she's going to fight me every step of the way.

What she doesn't understand is, I'm a Marine… and we never back down.

If we see a target we want… we take it.

It's as simple as that.

And I want her.

Badly.

RUTHLESS OBSESSION SERIES

A Dark Mafia Romance

Sweet Cruelty

Dimitri & Emma's story

It was an innocent mistake.

She knocked on the wrong door.

Mine.

If I were a better man, I would've just let her go.

But I'm not.

I'm a cruel bastard.

I ruthlessly claimed her virtue for my own.

It should have been enough.

But it wasn't.

I needed more.

Craved it.

She became my obsession.

Her sweetness and purity taunted my dark soul.

The need to possess her nearly drove me mad.

A Russian arms dealer had no business pursuing a naive librarian student.

She didn't belong in my world.

I would bring her only pain.

But it was too late…

She was mine and I was keeping her.

Sweet Depravity

Vaska & Mary's story

The moment she opened those gorgeous red lips to tell me no, she was mine.

I was a powerful Russian arms dealer and she was an innocent schoolteacher.

If she had a choice, she'd run as far away from me as possible.

Unfortunately for her, I wasn't giving her one.

I wasn't just going to take her; I was going to take over her entire world.

Where she lived.

What she ate.

Where she worked.

All would be under my control.

Call it obsession.

Call it depravity.

I don't give a damn… as long as you call her mine.

Sweet Savagery

Ivan & Dylan's Story

I was a savage bent on claiming her as punishment for her family's mistakes.

As a powerful Russian Arms dealer, no one steals from me and gets away with it.

She was an innocent pawn in a dangerous game.

She had no idea the package her uncle sent her from Russia contained my stolen money.

If I were a good man, I would let her return the money and leave.

If I were a gentleman, I might even let her keep some of it just for frightening her.

As I stared down at the beautiful living doll stretched out before me like a virgin sacrifice,

I thanked God for every sin and misdeed that had blackened my cold heart.

I was not a good man.

I sure as hell wasn't a gentleman… and I had no intention of letting her go.

She was mine now.

And no one takes what's mine.

Sweet Brutality

Maxim & Carinna's story

The more she fights me, the more I want her.

It's that beautiful, sassy mouth of hers.

It makes me want to push her to her knees and dominate her, like the brutal savage I am.

As a Russian Arms dealer, I should not be ruthlessly pursuing an innocent college student like her, but that would not stop me.

A twist of fate may have brought us together, but it is my twisted obsession that will hold her captive as my own treasured possession.

She is mine now.

I dare you to try and take her from me.

Sweet Ferocity

Luka & Katie's Story

I was a mafia mercenary only hired to find her, but now I'm going to keep her.

She is a Russian mafia princess, kidnapped to be used as a pawn in a dangerous territory war.

Saving her was my job. Keeping her safe had become my obsession.

Every move she makes, I am in the shadows, watching.

I was like a feral animal: cruel, violent, and selfishly out for my own needs. Until her.

Now, I will make her mine by any means necessary.

I am her protector, but no one is going to protect her from me.

IVANOV CRIME FAMILY TRILOGY

A Dark Mafia Romance

Savage Vow

Gregor & Samara's story

I took her innocence as payment.

She was far too young and naïve to be betrothed to a monster like me.

I would bring only pain and darkness into her sheltered world.

That's why she ran.

I should've just let her go…

She never asked to marry into a powerful Russian mafia family.

None of this was her choice.

Unfortunately for her, I don't care.

I own her… and after three years of searching… I've found her.

My runaway bride was about to learn disobedience has consequences… punishing ones.

Having her in my arms and under my control had become an obsession.

Nothing was going to keep me from claiming her before the eyes of God and man.

She's finally mine… and I'm never letting her go.

Vicious Oath

Damien & Yelena's story

When I give an order, I expect it to be obeyed.

She's too smart for her own good, and it's going to get her killed.

Against my better judgement, I put her under the protection of my powerful Russian mafia family.

So imagine my anger when the little minx ran.

For three long years I've been on her trail, always one step behind.

Finding and claiming her had become an obsession.

It was getting harder to rein in my driving need to possess her… to own her.

But now the chase is over.

I've found her.

Soon she will be mine.

And I plan to make it official, even if I have to drag her kicking and screaming to the altar.

This time… there will be no escape from me.

Betrayed Honor

Mikhail & Nadia's story

Her innocence was going to get her killed.

That was if I didn't get to her first.

She's the protected little sister of the powerful Ivanov Russian mafia family - the very definition of forbidden.

It's always been my job, as their Head of Security, to watch over her but never to touch.

That ends today.

She disobeyed me and put herself in danger.

It was time to take her in hand.

I'm the only one who can save her and I will fight anyone who tries to stop me, including her brothers.

Honor and loyalty be damned.

She's mine now.

For a list of All of Zoe Blake's Books Visit her Website!

www.zblakebooks.com

Printed in Great Britain
by Amazon